ALIEN SEAS

THE SCIENCE OFFICER: VOLUME 10

BLAZE WARD

KNOTTED ROAD PRESS

The Science Officer Series

The Science Officer

The Mind Field

The Gilded Cage

The Pleasure Dome

The Doomsday Vault

The Last Flagship

The Hammerfield Gambit

The Hammerfield Payoff

The Bryce Connection

Shadow of the Dominion

Longshot Hypothesis

Hard Bargain

Outermost

Dominion-427

Phoenix

Princess Rualoh

Hunter Bureau

Mirrors

Latency

Alien Seas
The Science Officer Volume 10
Blaze Ward
Copyright © 2020 Blaze Ward
All rights reserved
Published by Knotted Road Press
www.KnottedRoadPress.com

ISBN: 978-1-64470-185-0

Cover art:

ID 110797997 © Corey A Ford | Dreamstime.com

Cover and interior design copyright © 2020 Knotted Road Press

Reviews
It's true. Reviews help. Even a short one, such as, "Loved it!" So please consider reviewing this book (and all of the ones you've read) on your favorite retailer site.

Never miss a release!
If you'd like to be notified of new releases, sign up for my newsletter.

http://www.blazeward.com/newsletter/

Buy More!
Did you know that you can buy directly from my website?

https://www.blazeward.com/shop/

EXPLORER

PART ONE

"ALL AHEAD FULL," Zakhar gave the order as he looked out over his magnificent bridge, the kind you could have concerts or plays in. "Second star to the right, and straight on until morning."

"Excuse me?" Suvi popped up on the screen at his right hand like the piloting Yeoman she was, if she was seated in a different command space. Which she was.

Hers.

She was the ship. *Sentience-in-Residence* of the First-Rate-Galleon *Hammerfield*, the recovered derelict reclaimed and rechristened *Excalibur* for reasons that Zakhar didn't find nearly as funny as most of his command crew.

"Oh, like you weren't listening to the Neverland Overtures this morning, Miss Tinkerbell?" Zakhar teased.

For a creature that thought at more than 20,000 times the speed of a human, the lag as she stared at him was for his benefit more than anything. A recalcitrant teenager stewing and huffing, but only in their head lest they get in trouble with their commanding officer. He'd known a few of them in his career. Basic training didn't necessarily knock all that silliness out of a sailor.

"Fine," she sighed theatrically. "But you do understand that makes you Peter, right?"

"Hey, I don't wanna grow up, young lady, any more than you do or the rest of my lost boys and girls," Zakhar teased Suvi.

Zakhar smiled so wide it almost hurt. Around him, a dozen crewmembers suppressed giggles. Djamila returned the grin with the perfect eyeroll when he turned her direction, but she was just sitting and knitting this morning. As Dragoon—chief combat and security officer—she wouldn't have anything else to do for a while.

Suvi was a century or so older than he was, but presented as tall, blond, twenty-two-year-old of Finnish ancestry to his middle-aged Slavic bones. And acted like a teenage daughter to Javier, his Science Officer, and Zakhar's own niece.

It was weird, commanding a *Sentient* starship that was at least the equivalent of a Mark II Warmaster and acted occasionally like a goofball. But the original fairy had been a rather foul-mouthed creature.

Her modern incarnation hadn't lost anything in translation.

"I'll let you know when Hook and the pirates arrive," she replied in a dry tone that had everyone giggling, but the display on the big screen, just for him, began to shift as she brought the bow of the mighty explorer around and began to push.

Zakhar turned to his left and smiled at Javier. Technically, the man wasn't supposed to be on the bridge, but Zakhar didn't feel like ousting him today. They were here because of Javier. Simple as that.

The core of the crew still together, a former pirate family working out how to be law-abiding citizens again. They had a ship to sail, after his first love, the Strike Corvette *Storm Gauntlet* got killed in action by the pirates he and Javier eventually put paid to.

He even had love, glancing over at Djamila and wondering again what terrible things he must have suffered in a previous life to earn someone like her today.

Add in some financial backing and it was a new start.

A new day.

Tomorrow.

What was the term that Javier and Del had coined originally, before it bled out to the rest of the crew?

All possible tomorrows.

Yes, it was finally tomorrow. Zakhar Sokolov, former pirate and all-around evil dude, had a new lease on life. And he was going to take this chance and run with it as far and as long as he could.

There were whole chunks of the galaxy out there that nobody had done more than map with a telescope in so long that even most maps were marked with that most ancient of terms.

Here there be dragons.

Zakhar keyed the ship-wide intercom so everyone could hear him. The moment had that sort of feel to it. That sort of weight.

"All hands, this is the Captain," he said in a serious, sober tone that seemed to suck the silliness out of his bridge crew and his favorite fairy niece. "Stand by to transition to Jump. We've been planning this for a long time, and our time has finally come. I am glad you could all be here with me to enjoy it."

Zakhar paused and took a breath.

"Yeoman, take us to Jump."

Next stop, the alien suns.

PART TWO

JAVIER LOOKED up at the sound of a hatch opening. *The Lander* was currently parked in the main flight bay on *Excalibur* as he worked, perfectly flight-worthy, so his tinkering wasn't anything so much as something to do. A way to keep his skills sharp and focus him on something other than getting into trouble. A hobby he'd developed when Suvi was hidden in one of her old probes and needed work to keep them flying.

That he was working on the little shuttle's sensor also wouldn't come as a surprise to anyone that knew him. It was an old assault shuttle. Not as impressive as the nameless beast Del flew, the original assault shuttle parked just next door, but *The Lander* was cheap salvage that Javier had been able to buy and modify.

The inside portion of *The Lander* now was a specialized diving submarine. The outership could drop to the surface and hover in place while lowering the inner piece into the water. Del could them fly off anywhere and come back to pick them up later. Useful if you wanted to explore an entire world where most of the population lived underwater.

Javier pulled off his welding mask and studied Zakhar as the man entered the main cockpit and settled silently into the co-pilot's seat.

Javier supposed that the sensors could wait. Zakhar wouldn't have come here unless he wanted some privacy to talk. As much as you could get on a starship with a *Sentience* listening everywhere, but he didn't feel like telling her not to listen today.

Instead, he rested his helmet on the dash and took the pilot's station, trying not to read any weird symbolism into it.

They sat quiet for a few moments.

"It's a long flight to an unknown place, heading to *Ugen*," Zakhar mused aloud. "Many people might question the value of doing the thing."

"I could say *Because it's there*," Javier replied. "Many of the craziest accomplishments started that way."

"They did," Zakhar nodded, serenely Buddha-like in his chair. "And I've talked to others about the possibility of doing some good in the galaxy, to make up for all the evil."

"There is that," Javier nodded. "You and I, we've gotten a little notorious in a few places."

"And, as you like to remind people, they all had it coming," Zakhar replied. "But that's not why I'm here."

"Didn't figure," Javier said as a placeholder.

They lapsed into silence for a bit more time.

Javier had seen Zakhar Sokolov at his best. Possibly at his worst, as well. They had started as master and slave. Sultan and Janissary. But along the way they had gone somewhere else.

Brothers-in-Arms.

The Bryce Connection, linking two ex-*Concord* Navy officers together against the galaxy.

"How do you see *The Storm* shaping?" Zakhar finally asked.

They'd had the conversation a number of times, but always about the what and the when of the coming future. Rarely about the why.

"The *Concord* has been in charge for generations," Javier replied. "Accidental hegemon, maybe, but they took hold of that brass ring and held it tight. Seventy years ago nobody was in a position to argue with them. Not the *Union*, not *Balustrade*, certainly not *Neu Berne*. You got to be one of the good guys helping hold the galaxy together."

"You as well," Zakhar retorted.

"Only barely," Javier shrugged. "Class of '49 versus my class of '63. Not quite a generation there, but most of my career was on the other side of some mark a historian like Bethany Durbin could draw separating eras. After the calm, perhaps."

"*The Rising Storm*?" the man asked, his face growing serious.

"As good a name as any," Javier agreed. "Eventually, they'll agree on a term, but looking at some of the books she's found for me, I figure it started being recognized in about 567. The rise of piracy more recently, folks like you just represented the breakdown of the systems that had been keeping the general peace. Fleets got cut down hard by bureaucrats and populations tired of paying taxes because they couldn't see the value derived."

"Nobody ever looks beyond the corner store," Zakhar agreed. "They see the price of milk and chips go up. Or the sales tax increase, however much. Inflation eats at their savings. Some politician comes along and promises to make it all better, without ever explaining the hard choices that have to be made."

"Because they'll long-since be out of office by the time those bills come due," Javier nodded. "So you have a lot of sailors on the dock now. Old warships being stored against future need, but it's cheaper to sell them off to someone than it is to melt them down or keep them in storage. Pirates start hitting the fringes of organized space between nations, rather than anywhere important. Local systems ask for help, and when it isn't coming, they have to strike off on their own. Personally, I'm surprised that the *Union of Man* still has as many planets as it does, but I suppose there are enough other places to bother that they've managed to hold on longer."

"But it's going to change?" Zakhar asked.

"That's Bethany's expertise," Javier said. "But I have traveled to a lot of places. You see a number of stations that haven't had a new coat of paint in too long. Fleets and navies being stretched far and away beyond what they were designed for, because there is no budget to replace and upgrade systems regularly. Same with ships. Nobody is a military threat, so why do you need battle squadrons sailing around?"

"Yeah, piracy was always seen as a local issue," Zakhar said. "I could sail beyond anyone's jurisdiction, even today, because folks don't get along well enough to cooperate. *Neu Berne* is still culturally pissed at everyone. The *Union of Man* is living in a fantasy of the good old days when they were the most powerful nation in history. *Balustrade* is always one week from another revolution of some sort. So why bother, Javier? Why do this difficult and expensive thing?"

"I want to be remembered for trying, Zakhar," Javier turned now to look squarely at the man. "I may not make the galaxy any better, but if I set an example, maybe someone along the way will see that and decide it is a good thing. I'll remind you that Suvi is going to outlive us both by hopefully centuries, depending on how people view *Sentiences* in the future."

"But we might not succeed?"

"*I tried* is the most powerful phrase in the history of humanity, Zakhar," Javier said. "You don't have to succeed. You can fail miserably. Die to the last man. Something. But the 47 Ronin are as immortal as Leonidas and his Three Hundred."

"Because they tried," Zakhar said.

"Yes," Javier agreed. "And so The Science Officer is also going to try."

PART THREE

Javier sat at his bridge station and looked down at the planet *Ugen* with a jaundiced eye.

From space, it was a pretty blue marble, but he wasn't fooled. Not one bit.

Shallow seas covered something like ninety percent of the planetary surface. And shallow was the key here. According to sensors that were sharp enough to pierce the cloud layer and lay those secrets below bare, more than seventy percent of all oceans on *Ugen* were less than one hundred meters deep. Too much for an unprotected human to dive, but more than enough to trap heat and absorb it. Channel it up to the surface.

The planet had fantastic coral reefs.

And monumental typhoons.

He was tracking six of them visible, just on the eighth of the planet that he could see.

Nobody important was being threatened by them, but that was because the locals were smart enough not to live on the surface of their planet.

A few were in orbit. The system had a pretty sophisticated customs setup aboard a massive orbital platform that was far bigger than a population of less than one hundred million people needed.

But he'd also read all the tourism brochures that they had

picked up as they got closer, doing port calls at places like *Dreely* and *Goli Thofa* to buy supplies. With that much water, there was always a perfect beach somewhere you could set down and enjoy.

The key was landing in your own shuttle and being able to take off again immediately when the weather changed. That or just climbing into your family submarine and returning to one of the massive underwater domes where most of the people lived.

A lot of the population were spacers, but that made perfect sense. You had to be comfortable in small spaces without access to sky in both instances. And the planet had been terraformed early on. Thirty-fifth Century, if the records were to be believed, so the fish had had something like four thousand years now to evolve and adapt. Same with crustaceans and everybody else.

Ugen supported itself just fine on aquaculture, both fish and various flora. If the world hadn't had five monster supernovas in neighborhood before *Ugen*'s star had formed, they would still be rich, just exporting fish.

But those supernovae had left all sorts of wonderfully exotic stuff under the surface. And shallow oceans.

The people had largely been protected by those same oceans, even as various wars had raged around them. The Resource Wars had been a threat, with several neighbors arguing over the planet for centuries. The Corporate Wars had actually been so horribly bad in other places that *Ugen* was largely ignored. During the Pocket Empires Era, they had almost been forgotten and not much had changed across the *Union of Man* Era or the wars over the last five hundred years.

Which was why Javier had convinced the Khatum that it was safe to let him sail a quarter of the way around the galaxy on an adventure. And bring all his friends with him.

Javier looked up from his screens, feeling a pair of eyes on him.

Bethany Marie Durbin. Bryce Academy graduate, Class of '79.

Damn, he was old. Not as old at Zakhar's class of '49, but his own class of '63 made him a relic around this woman.

Which was part of the reason why he'd hired her.

Her face had a relaxed look. Intrigued, but not enough to just poke him to get his attention. He was still working on that part, but she was a librarian, both by vocation and temperament.

Quiet.

"Talk to me, kid," Javier said.

He could do that. She was almost young enough to be his daughter.

Somewhere behind him, Javier heard Zakhar snort quietly.

"You always say that there is a storm coming," Bethany began quietly, one hand up and gesturing to the space around them, and presumably the entire known galaxy, which was a significant portion of this side of the disk.

Nobody knew about the other side. Folks had theoretically circumnavigated by now, but Javier hadn't seen any maps of the back side of the Central Core.

That was the next adventure after this mission, assuming he could talk Behnam into it. Suvi'd be all in, as would a significant chunk of the crew. Assuming he could talk Chay and Burdine into it, he'd even have his favorite French restaurant with him.

"A storm is coming," Javier assured Bethany.

She nodded, making a face that suggested they were about to talk about "*Why?*".

"I've been studying all the stuff we've picked up along the way, so I can decipher it for you and Suvi," she continued. "*Ugen*'s about as safe a place as you are likely to find, unless someone is committed to destroying planets with orbital bombardment."

Javier nodded. He'd drawn the same conclusion, but it was nice having an expert confirm that. And Bethany was an expert. A historian recommended to Javier by his old Professor of Political History, Dorn Hetzel.

"There's going to be another war, Bethany," Javier said, pitching his voice a little louder so the others could hear it.

Zakhar sat at the center of the grand cathedral of a bridge. Seriously, Javier had commanded starships that were smaller.

Heads craned a little in his direction. They did that when he felt like talking.

Djamila Sykora, Ship's Dragoon. All 2.1 meters of her badass self. Mary-Elizabeth Suzuki, Gunner. Piet Alferdinck, Pilot. Kibwe Bousaid, Executive Assistant to the Captain. Tobias Gibney, Backup Gunner and technically the vessel's Science Officer, since they'd gone and promoted Javier's sorry ass to Ambassador for crimes he should have committed.

"*Altai* is far too removed from *Ugen* to make them a trade partner to the Khatum," Bethany pointed out. "It would be like Rome and Nanjing trading via overland caravans of camels, back on the homeworld, when you might spend the better part of a year getting between the two. Way before they discovered the Cape of Good Hope or dug the canal at Sinai."

Again, he nodded. History had never been his gig, with his dreams and hijinks down in the biological sciences building, but he understood her words at an instinctive level.

And Javier liked the way she'd said *We* in referring to the crew of former pirates around her. Most of them had accepted *Altai* citizenship as part of the gig. It gave them a place where there were currently no warrants out for their arrest and the Khatum wouldn't extradite anyone.

If you pissed her off that bad, she'd just kill you herself.

"Rome and Nanjing," Javier agreed. "Two ends of an impossibly long trade route, right?"

Bethany nodded, still unsure as to the "Why?" question.

"Something would have to be incredibly valuable to be worth hauling that far?" Javier continued, noting the other unconscious nods around him. "And no single ship would haul it that incredible distance, most likely, so they'd haul things to a second point, closer. Then someone else would haul it another step of the way. Eventually, it does get there, but it has to pass through a lot of hands first."

"Thereby establishing a network of interested traders who know what goods to transmit up and down the line. The ancient

Silk Road on *Earth*," Bethany breathed out the words, understanding finally coming to her face. She turned to Zakhar now. "Is he always like this?"

The bridge crew laughed, including the projection of Suvi everyone had on a side screen at their stations.

"I've learned to trust the man when he gets serious," Zakhar replied soberly. "Even if the dork is usually a goofball."

More laughter. It felt good to Javier to hear it. He could still remember dreaming about having them all hung from a high yardarm in low gravity, back when they first met, five years ago.

Bethany grew serious now as he watched. Introverted in a way that maybe only he and Piet understood. The rest were too loud, most of the time.

"Spider web," Bethany finally said, nodding to herself. "*Altai* to *Ugen*. Where's the next anchor point around the outer ring?"

Javier smiled. Probably nobody else on this vessel was trained enough to figure his logic out. They were all smart, but none of them were Historians.

"*Muhua Bara*," Javier answered, just to watch her face screw up sideways in confusion.

"Not funny, Javier," Suvi spoke out of every speaker, just so everyone heard her. "Bethany, that's a theoretical place, not a real world. I found a reference to it in an ancient Gazetteer article, but that was a terraforming and colonizing report three thousand years old. Nobody knows exactly where it is or if there's a colony there."

"Where it is?" The historian turned to Suvi's image now.

Bethany had light brown hair that couldn't decide if it was dirty blond or mousy brown, and dark blue eyes, so she and Suvi almost looked like cousins, depending.

Except that Suvi was the AI that ran the ship, rather than flesh and blood. Still as real as the rest of them, though.

"On the other side of the Galactic Core," Suvi answered. "Almost one hundred and thirty degrees anti-spinward from *Altai*, out along the Scutum-Centaurus Arm, if my idiot cousins are to be believed."

"Cousins?" Bethany asked.

"The original survey and terraforming vessels were hyper-intelligent computers," Suvi said. "Brute force logic machines without a full neural network capable of leaping to conclusions or reprogramming themselves. Just send them out without risking human lives and hope they came back later. True AI sentience only came about much later. Much more recently."

"Hey, the station finally noticed us and sent a hail," Tobias broke in at this point. "Sounds like a call the Ambassador should take."

Javier groaned as everyone else laughed. Tobias grinned, but that was just an excuse to get Javier off his bridge and let the man do his job.

"Fine," Javier shut things down and rose. "I'll take it in the main conference room. Someone route it over, please?"

Laughter followed him out of the room and into the main hallway, but he couldn't fault them. Many of those people had gone from his keepers to his comrades to his friends when they weren't looking.

Now he had to pull an even bigger swindle on the folks of *Ugen*.

PART FOUR

Looking around the shuttle interior, Djamila kept her grin to herself. Javier wouldn't appreciate how thoroughly she had gotten inside his head until he looked around.

He was the only male present. She could have thrown his harmony off by bringing one of the so-called Gun Bunnies, all of whom were currently male, but had resisted the temptation and only brought her pathfinders, Sascha and Hajna. To which had been added Dr. Rainier St. Kitts and her wife, Dr. Emma St. Kitts. Bethany Durbin. Afia Burakgazi.

Djamila hadn't inquired of the rumor mill if Javier had ever slept with the new Historian, like he had her pathfinders and Afia. The St. Kitts's didn't like boys at all, and she'd have to be blackout drunk to even consider it.

But Javier's so-called ground team were all female. All utterly competent and capable, or she would have brought more killers with her.

Maybe Djamila needed to go recruiting and find Javier a whole harem of lethal gun molls, just to mess with him? He'd started off with 'Mina Teague in the role of Hadiiye, back when the two of them had come to rescue her from Abraam Tamaz. Djamila had filled that role at *Shang-du* after Teague departed although she had no interest in ever sleeping with the man. Still, the man liked to be surrounded by competent women.

Even the pilot of this shuttle was female, judging from her voice from behind the cockpit door. Pity that Del hadn't been able to fly them, but the locals insisted on using their own systems, unwilling to trust a stranger to land on the deck of a pitching oceanic vessel. Plus, *Excalibur*'s assault shuttle was much larger, so it might not fit down there.

Still, she smiled.

In a galactic age that had seen men become dominant again, Javier was sticking it to the world in his own way.

"All hands, stand by for terminal maneuvers," the pilot announced from up front in a throaty alto voice. "We will be landing in ninety seconds, so keep your harness intact until I send a green light."

Nobody had moved to unbuckle back here, but Djamila assumed that the woman was used to dealing with tourists and civilians. Nobody aboard *Excalibur* were really amateurs, as they were all used to deep space by now. And both her and Emma had pounded into people all the lessons of surviving space travel and following orders during the now-thrice-weekly exercise programs Dr. St. Kitts had brought with her when she joined the crew.

Djamila called up an image of the exterior on a small screen close to her station.

The vessel below was a long, semi-flattened cylinder turned on its side, with a pointed nose that dropped back into shoulders on both sides. The top was flat and marked with landing circles behind a conning tower.

Everything was smooth and rounded, and she could see vertical fins coming out of the water aft, marking impellors. A submarine shuttle carrier. Certainly novel, but she supposed that if nobody lived on the surface of the world, you would need something like this to allow people to come and go.

Excalibur had a modified assault shuttle that could drop a submarine from its center, but most people would be reliant on the locals to get around.

They landed, the thruster blowing a spray of salt water in all directions. Almost as soon as the shuttle shut down its engines, a dome behind the conning tower hinged open, like the mouth of a crocodile, and a small truck wheeled out.

Two people attached a tow hitch quickly and then got back into the truck. Djamila watched on her screen as they were pulled into the beast's maw. An elevator lowered them a deck and then the truck pushed the shuttle backwards and expertly into a parking slot, next to three others already present.

"All hands, we have arrived," the pilot called over the intercom. "Please look about your seating area for any items you might have brought aboard as you make your way aftward. It has been our pleasure transporting you today and we look forward to seeing you again on your next trip. Thanks for flying *Ugen* Airways."

They were all unbuckling. Djamila shut her screen down and rose.

Outside, a steward of some sort got them onto the wet deck and through an airlock door, down a long hallway, and into a lounge area that had an automat delivering food and several flavors of drink, both hot and cold.

Javier had local currency for everyone, so a few gathered around to get coffee or tea, but she went forward to the rounded bow, where she could see the underside of the ocean through the transparent panel.

"All passengers be prepared for movement," another voice announced. This one sounded recorded. "Dive imminent. Drinks and food may spill."

Ten seconds of panic passed for the rest, and then the engines started up with a hard purr Djamila could feel in her feet. The bow inclined slightly and the vessel dove beneath the waves.

It wasn't a trap, per se, but she felt herself at someone else's mercy. It would only get worse when they reached the city itself, a dome hidden deep beneath the waves.

PART FIVE

From an engineering perspective, Afia wasn't all that impressed. Tech to build a dome city underwater was older than dirt, but the pretty vids and books always left out the constant level of maintenance you had to do to keep crap from growing on it. Hell, barnacles and stuff would just see it as another reef to build on, and you couldn't do much without poisoning all your local water pretty damned quick.

I it was up to her, she's have gone straight down into the bedrock and just piped in views of the ocean floor to every room like they did on a station. But she understood why they didn't do that.

It would be too oppressive to the spirit, even though the mines were three quarters of the reason folks lived on this rock.

Same problem there, though. Too much pollution digging and you ended up running out of food quick. Or growing a physical eye instead of just opening the metaphysical one.

They hadn't done something like this on *Terra*, but you didn't need to with a population of two billion and that much land. Plus, folks feeling the need could just emigrate to places like this, same same. Wasn't all that far, as spaceships went.

Galaxy apart culturally.

She'd once taken a vacation to the Caribbean with the

family. Totally different from her family's home in the Yukon Protectorate. Too hot. Too bright. But the same, glorious blue.

Terra was ancient. The home of humans. *Ugen* was a place folks had come to.

Still, they were here. She'd heard all Javier's plans and gambits. Thought they were nuts, but hey, it was Javier. Afia had done weirder with the man over the years.

Folks stirred as they got close, a domed city glowing in the trench as they came over a rock ledge now and pitched the bow over.

Again, silly design, submarine taxis and all. She'd have just floated an elevator shaft to a dock on the surface for tourists. If nobody had done that, Afia had to wonder how many tourists they really got from outsystem. Maybe the marketing crap was just a load of hooey?

The hurricanes couldn't be that bad, could they?

She was here. They'd look at stuff. Do deals. Drink heavily. Maybe dance too much. At some point, Afia was looking forward to an afternoon on a warm beach with nothing but sunscreen on.

"You don't seem impressed." Javier was suddenly beside her.

Damn, he moved quiet when he wanted to. Still had it, even if he was on the far side of forty now and starting to finally look mature in ways that still carbonated her hormones when she thought nobody was looking.

"Better ways to engineer it," Afia shrugged, glancing around. All the others were stirring, but generally watching a big screen over her head that presumably had a zoom and some cleanup going to cut the fuzziness of the water.

"And?" he asked, leadingly.

"Chesterton's Fence," Afia turned just enough to watch him get confused.

She lived for that. For pulling a fast one on The Science Officer. Even when she had to have Suvi's help looking up something Afia just barely remembered. But the Ship-Chick was one of the coolest people Afia knew.

Javier thought for a long beat and then shrugged.

"Still don't get it," he said. "Explanation?"

"So you see a fence, and someone has built it across the road, which is stupid," Afia grinned. "First impulse is to say *Let's tear it down and make this more efficient*. But that's a bad idea. Chesterton said so."

"Why is it bad?" Javier asked.

"Someone had a reason to put it there in the first place," Afia answered. "Maybe their reason for having it makes more sense than your reason for removing it. So you gotta ask them. Find out what they were about. Engineers are trained to think that way, but somebody forgot the dude's name along the way."

"Chesterton," Javier noted. "Starship architect or something?"

"Old priest," Afia laughed. "Pre-starflight *Terra*."

"So you don't like the design of the city…?"

"But they had a reason for doing it, so I need to listen." She turned now and grinned up at the guy. "You know how important it is to listen when someone has *needs*…"

Damn, he really blushed.

Afia nearly giggled. They'd been occasional lovers, but not since the Khatum. Afia wondered if he was truly that much in love, or just saving himself for later. She would not turn down a midnight knock on her door from the man, even as she doubted it would be coming anytime soon.

Maybe she needed to find one of the locals who was all that and a bag of chips and ride him like a pony.

Javier cleared his throat, which seemed to be a way of underlining an end to that part of the conversation. The Dragoon was approaching, merriment present in her eyes if you knew where to look.

Djamila still didn't understand poker, but that was okay. Afia had three sharps in view right now if she felt like putting a game together and cleaning out some locals who thought they understood cards.

"Ambassador, you should prepare," Djamila announced in a quiet voice with just the perfect pitch of subservient bimbo to it.

Afia wondered who had taught the Amazon babe that trick, because Javier blushed AGAIN.

Damn, twice in one week? What was the world coming to?

He left, grumbling. Djamila took his spot. Afia felt like a pixie, coming up to about the woman's boobs. *Pixie Kodiak*, of course, which is what her brother had taken to calling her, way back when.

"Thoughts?" Afia asked, mostly to see what the woman was about today. Totally different creature than the Dragoon Afia had originally met, back before Javier.

Blame him for everything. Him and 'Mina.

"I always wonder when he's finally going to get in over his head," Sykora mused.

"We might be there now," Afia offered, causing the giant woman to turn her whole body her way and shift into combat mode like someone had just flipped a switch.

"How?"

"Look around," Afia gestured to the room. "He only usually takes as much force as he needs to do a job, and no more. Like robbing the Khatum that first time. This time, he brought an awful lot of folks for what's supposed to be merely a trade mission."

"Oh," Djamila noted, her tone far more serious now. "What are you expecting?"

"I have no clue," Afia replied honestly. "But neither does he, and that's what worries me."

PART SIX

Suvi turned her face to the sun and just drank in mana from heaven.

Humans didn't understand that feeling, except for maybe Afia, if the comparisons held water.

Suvi felt solar wind caress every square centimeter of her body. Heard the gas giants and the sun groaning and beeping and howling at each other across the cold darkness.

Closer in, there was a station. Huge place, similar in size to *Meehu Platform*, which was far more than this world needed. But all the processing smelters were there, where everything was handled. And most of the rock that was leftover wasn't shoved out an airlock to plummet to the surface below, like on most worlds. A bunch of it was shipped off to various stations and outposts around here, either in system or one of the nearby stars, where it got traded for stuff and then turned into dirt.

Seriously, according to the public records, less than two hundred tons of material was returned to the planetary surface in any given year. Most of that was the nasty stuff that nobody wanted or could use for anything else, so it went back into one of the dead mines as filler, generally encased in glass with an expected half-life longer than humanity.

She watched a shuttle lifting off from the surface in an elaborate choreography, hauling a load of stuff in a pod that it would dump when it got to the station, like a tiny dump truck. The economy must be doing good, because she saw four others out there in other stages of their delicate minuet.

For not having much population, this place had a lot of traffic.

Suvi studied the logs again for several hours of personaltime as a thought struck her. Where had she seen that record?

Her mind was a library. She spent time just wandering until she found the book she wanted, and then envisioned a chair so she could sit and read it.

And a mint julep, because it felt like a mint julep kind of day and nobody was going to complain about her drinking before noon.

As the ancient Royal Navy had once said: Drinking on duty was fine, as long as one was not rendered unfit for duty due to drink.

It was a really good mint julep, because she could make it perfect.

Aha!

Crap!

I hate being right sometimes.

Who to tell?

Technically, she should alert Tobias, since he was now officially the Science Officer in charge of sensors with Javier off gallivanting. And he was a nice enough guy, she supposed. Maybe.

Not nearly as salty as Del, or as much fun as Adrian or Ilan. What to do?

Fine, it was going there anyway. Let's just tell the boss.

PART SEVEN

ZAKHAR LOOKED up as the screen on the wall lit up with a *Concord* Navy logo. The sound of knocking emanated from the speakers.

Even though it was her starship, her body, the girl had been raised *Concord* Navy, and those things went bone deep. Especially for a *Sentience*.

"Enter," Zakhar said in response.

"Captain," Suvi appeared on the screen and saluted smartly.

Ayumu Ulfsson, her first captain, had been something of a stickler for that sort of behavior. Zakhar was still working on breaking her down to something a little more casual.

Not as much as when she was dealing with Javier, but a little less spit and polish at times. Something appropriate for a group of pirates going straight, maybe.

"What can I do for you, Yeoman?" Zakhar asked, himself also falling back into the old patterns.

"I'm routing you a report I just analyzed, sir," she said, still prim with her shoulders back and her head up. "I believe it has implications."

At the speed that woman thought, he wondered how many days would pass for her before he could read it. But Zakhar also knew that he was only dealing with a single shard of her whole awareness right now.

He picked up his handheld and keyed it on. It beeped with a message and Zakhar opened the attachment.

An Analysis of Orbital Traffic Patterns: Crime and Smuggling in the Modern Age.

Interesting.

"Critical paragraph?" he asked.

Instead of answering, she bounced the document in to a graphic showing a set of curves in different colors.

"And what does the local grid look like?" Zakhar asked her anyway.

It was obvious what she had seen, but he wanted her to get into the habit of not reading his mind.

"We are seeing local orbital traffic in line with the scenario in green, sir," Suvi replied. "One and a half standard deviations above normal. Estimate seventy percent reliability."

Zakhar flipped the document back to the beginning and checked the title page. Copyright 4744 CE. Deep in the Resource Wars Era, when smuggling might have been at an all-time high for the species.

And three thousand years ago, which meant the conclusions were suspect. But she would know that. It was right out at the edge of being a statistical abnormality.

Suvi was smart enough to know that, too.

But it niggled at him.

"Spin up a shard and dedicate it to analyzing local traffic patterns with passive transponders," Zakhar ordered. "Hard ping the system every six to nine hours on a semi-random basis and feed those results in as well, expecting people running under the same sort of cloak that *Storm Gauntlet* used to have. Remind me daily to check your plots against these grids for correlation."

"Aye aye, sir," she replied brightly.

As she vanished, Zakhar supposed that maybe Suvi was feeling like she was back in the fleet again, too, to be thinking such thoughts. It was their little secret, the two of them pretending to be *Concord* Navy once more, when they were both past their time and retired. Javier didn't have it in him, and

Bethany Durbin was too busy learning how to be a civilian these days to want to play.

He wasn't worried about the ship itself. After her refit, nothing less than a Class III Warmaster was even a threat on the physical level.

But he had a team of people down on the surface.

Zakhar considered sending them a warning, but Javier had Djamila and Afia with him.

How dangerous could it get?

AMBASSADOR

PART ONE

JAVIER HAD to hand it to Behnam. There was a world of difference between showing up as a random spacer bribing high officers with fresh fruit, and a credentialed Ambassador from a foreign land, come bearing gifts and offering trade.

If nothing else, the food at the reception banquets was so much better. Like now. Heavy on fish, naturally, and sea vegetables, but someone had a greenhouse down here with enough oomph that he'd seen Rainier St. Kitts's eyebrows go up. And meat got imported from somewhere else, since you didn't have space for anything but factory veal.

Oh sure, chickens in the greenhouse made sense. Double crop and improved output. But goat? Lamb? Water buffalo?

Two bars, neither of them cash-based. And a separate coffee bar serving things derived from hot water pressed through seeds, leaves, and other stuff.

A man could get used to this.

Maybe fifty or seventy people, not counting servers working the room. Big picture window looking out over the water with lights on, both close and in the distance, showing the odd fish swimming by.

"Enjoying yourself, Ambassador Aritza?" a casual voice came up over his shoulder.

Javier still found it weird not having at least one gun moll killer babe with a handy pistol standing within arm's reach, but glancing to his left he saw Djamila watching as she politely fended off what appeared to be only a semi-serious proposition from a fat man in a nice suit.

And both Sascha and Hajna were around, if things got weird. Dressed in their best slinky dresses, the way he liked them, as a cover and disguise, although Javier doubted they were fooling anybody serious.

He turned to greet the newcomer.

Andak Luo. Merchant Prince of *Ugen*, for lack of a better term. No aristocratic rank around here, but a handful of extremely old families maintaining a polite competition with each other, and then marrying over every couple of generations to prevent another Romeo and Juliet scenario.

At least one hoped.

Javier was too jaded to think the species had actually learned anything in the last six thousand years.

But the man was impressive. Charismatic in a way that made him seem taller, larger than he really was, when he was perhaps a centimeter shorter than Javier. Not as broad or physically fit, but Javier's native laziness had met its match in Behnam and Emma St. Kitts's orders about his daily workout regimens.

Dark hair verging on black, but looking natural rather than chemically-induced. Appealing, rugged face that would have the women swooning if he ratcheted up the charm another notch. Maybe fifty years standard.

Expensive suit with a sheen and texture that looked like someone had somehow turned silk into sharkskin.

But the man had asked him a question.

"Eminently so, sir," Javier replied with a slight bow.

The *Concord* Navy pounded deportment in so deep that you could be charming and suave even when dead drunk. Javier had proved it more than once.

"I'm given to understand that you and Fritz Bamanie represent the two largest export firms on the planet?" Javier asked.

Bethany had done a LOT of homework as they had approached *Ugen*, buying books for the ship's library with a budget that had made her alternately blush and gulp.

But Javier was playing a game measured in centuries. Millennia, even. Knowledge lost was gone forever, but if you stored it in a good library and hired a *Sentience* to keep track of everything, then nothing might ever actually vanish.

"That would be an accurate assessment, Ambassador," Luo replied. "Might I be so bold as to inquire what brings you such a tremendous distance from your own fabled homeland?"

Javier grinned. You could always tell when someone was getting ready to bullshit you by how flowery their language got. How many extra syllables were suddenly necessary to communicate the same ideas.

Still, he might as well see what the fellow was about.

Jacks or better to open, considering the table and the stakes around here.

"Curiosity, on one hand," Javier said. "*Altai* is more than ninety degrees of ascension around the rim, so we rarely hear any news of the older sectors, except what filters through *Concord* space."

"Indeed," the man nodded. "*Ugen* is rather isolated, both geographically as well as our own style of living, so we rarely hear news from outside the sector as well. But that was only part of your purpose?"

And perceptive as hell. Mustn't forget that part.

"Trade," Javier smiled now. "My boss, the Khatum of *Altai* herself, is interested in establishing trade relations with many distant places. Stars that are almost alien to us, to help foster the growth of specialized routes. *Ugen* struck us as a good starting point, because you are the most unique world my researchers were able to identify."

"How so?" Luo asked. "Many worlds have significant submarine cultures. We're hardly special in that way."

"In your distant past, at least five supernovae seeded nearby space with heavy elements in significant and complicated quantities," Javier gestured at the invisible sky above the oceans over their heads. "And each had a different spectrographic fingerprint at the time of death, so the mix around here is extremely exotic and far and away greater than almost any planet my research could locate. *Ugen* sat as close to the center as you can get, comparing the stellar remains, so was quintuply blessed."

"You seem to know your sciences, Ambassador," Luo responded leadingly.

"Oh, that's to be expected," Javier let his face fall into a smile as he spoke. "While my PhD work at King's College on *Altai* was recent, I had a significant career as a Science Officer, both in *Concord* service and later in civilian life."

"I see." Luo's face got cagey now. "Then perhaps you would appreciate a tour of one of our mines? To get a better feel for how we do things on *Ugen*?"

"I was actually trying to figure out how to sneak or bribe my way aboard one of your mining subs," Javier admitted with a grin. "But that's the nerdy side of me forgetting that I can just ask. Still getting used to being an Ambassador, you know."

Luo pulled a card from inside his jacket and handed it to Javier.

"This has my personal contact information on it, Ambassador Aritza," he said. "Please do not hesitate to contact me when you would like to have a picnic. Now, I have taken up perhaps too much of your time, and see others circling, so I shall step back for now."

The man bowed and literally stepped back with a knowing grin on his face before turning back to the crowd around them and departing.

Javier studied the thing in his hand. After however many centuries of computer communications, it was still a small piece of card stock. Off white. Maybe paper, maybe a form of polymer better designed to withstand water immersion. Not as big as a playing card, rather thinner.

Andak Luo. Several contact methods. No title. Corporate logo for Luo Industrial Products in one corner.

He slipped it into a pocket as the other great power of *Ugen* approached.

Andak Luo was probably about fifty, according to various published reports. Fritz Bamanie was somewhere past sixty now.

Darker and more florid than Luo, or even Javier's Hispanic heritage, but not all the way down into part of the African Diaspora, which emigration records suggested were fairly rare in this sector of space. Rail thin and short.

Javier might have suggested Napoleonic, but the man didn't have that edge of madness or the chip on his shoulders that others might have carried.

"I see the competition has been in trying to steal a march," Bamanie said with a wry smile as he stepped up.

The man had a deeper voice than you would expect from such a small frame. Baritone verging down into bass if he sang in a choir. Or the shower.

"Perhaps," Javier replied with a smile. "Low grade industrial espionage, at a minimum."

"Ah, good," Bamanie said, sticking his hand out. "Fritz."

"Javier." He shook.

"So I should have my spies steal everything from his spies when he writes it up?" Fritz chuckled.

"Certainly a useful exercise for everyone involved," Javier grinned. "Keep them on their toes, if the big boss is showing them up from time to time."

"Spies can be lazy folk," Fritz leaned close to confide with a knowing nod. "That was how I got to be in charge."

"I thought you were the only child of the previous chair?" Javier offered, showing the man he had done his homework. "The sole heir to a controlling interest?"

"Piffle," Fritz waved a hand negligently. "I have uncles and cousins who could have made a stink, but they hired lazy spies."

"I see," Javier nodded. "And what would they have found?"

Fritz actually looked both ways with a lascivious grin.

"Can't tell you," he murmured. "Statute of limitations on relevant lawsuits hasn't run out yet."

Javier laughed. This man was also a bullshit artist, but a much more interesting one.

Fritz joined the laughter.

"So, Fritz," Javier asked. "What does *Ugen* Export Services sell?"

"What would you like to buy?" the man volleyed the question back immediately with a wicked grin.

Call. Raise. Call.

"My ship has significant cargo capacity, but not that much," Javier noted dryly. "This is a trade mission, rather than a merchant caravan, but we'd like to see about setting up a few of those."

"My conglomerate pretty much has a tentacle in any industry an advanced economy like this requires," Fritz replied. "The planet exports fish and rock. Pick your flavor and your destination."

"Who has the most processing smelter capacity in orbit?" Javier asked, deciding to test the man.

"Damned good question," Fritz answered, rocking back on his heels a little. "It's Tuesday, so I think Andak does."

"It will change by Friday?"

"Sunday, I'm sure," Fritz grinned. "We pretty much run things constantly, but breakdowns and maintenance have around ten percent of our total capacity off line at any time. Lot of people shopping for exotic metals this season."

"Exotic?" Javier asked, intrigued now.

"Iron and nickel are like the third and fifth most common elements you'll find in any planetary system worth its salt," Fritz replied. "Common. *Ugen* has the weird shit in spades, shallow enough that we can dig it out, lift it to orbit for smelting, and ship it across the sector cheaper than someone else can turn asteroids into the same bar stock, because we don't have to do the hard processing stuff with our ore. It comes premade into exotics, just needing to be cracked and poured."

"Ship much to the *Concord?*" Javier pressed, surprised at the depth of information this man had at his fingertips.

"Not particularly," Fritz shrugged. "I'd have to review a

quarterly report, but they might barely be in the top ten export markets. Too far and they have closer strategic mines. *Da Xing* and *Arsinoe* are my top markets.

"*Arsinoe?*" Javier was shocked. "The pirate world?"

Fritz laughed.

"We're all pirates, Javier," he replied. "I presume they are just a warehousing front for neighbors. The *Union of Man*, or what's left of it. Maybe *Balustrade*."

Javier refrained from explaining to the man how recently he'd been a pirate. Hopefully nobody around here would ever hear stories of what Captain Navarre did to Walvisbaai Industrial with an old, *Neu Berne* First Rate Galleon like the one currently in orbit.

One of the only such vessels still in service, anywhere in the galaxy, at that.

"Besides, those fine folks on *Arsinoe*, their money spends just as well as everyone else's," Fritz said. "So how can I bribe the Ambassador from *Altai?*"

That latter was said with humor, but there was a serious tone underneath. Like everything up to now had just been a long sneak to get close.

At least the man was comradery itself.

"Luo is taking me on one of his subs to see a mine at some point," Javier said sideways. "Maybe a tour of your smelters? And also any greenhouse you've got. I'm a botanist, and so is the brunette Dr. St. Kitts."

Javier grinned as Fritz's eyes crossed slightly. He rarely introduced himself as Dr. Aritza, but both women rather insisted on being Dr. St. Kitts. At least around strangers.

"There," Javier pointed to Rainier. "Talking to Sykora."

As if anybody could miss the Amazon, half a head taller than anybody else in the room right now.

"Botanists?" Fritz asked. From his tone, it sounded like he thought someone was playing a prank on him.

"Indeed," Javier grinned. "I first met Rainier in relation to the Seed Vaults at *Svalbard*."

Where he had been all set to hijack her ship when

everybody got captured by a whole 'nother group of pirates, before he rescued her from said pirates with the help of Suvi and Djamila Sykora, then proceeded to blow up a major pirate base as payback.

After which he had sought out Rainier St. Kitts because he needed help breeding his dreamberries back from where he'd screwed up.

Simple stuff.

"You have the advantage on me then," Fritz said with a hint of bemusement to his tone. "But I'm sure I can find something interesting. What is Dr. St. Kitt's specialization?"

"Fruit, generally," Javier said. "She and I have consulted on a variety of breeding programs along those lines."

Javier knew he was being a shit, but he enjoyed that look of utter blank shock that came across people's faces when they realized that *The Ambassador From Altai* wasn't just another pretty face. That he was a former *Concord* science officer who knew plants.

And chickens.

"Obviously, then, this will need to expand into a much greater conspiracy than I had anticipated," Fritz finally grinned after a moment, wheels in his head turning from the look in his eyes. "I shall endeavor to make it worth your while, Javier."

The man took his leave and Javier maneuvered himself over for some tea, humming a piraty ditty as he did.

"What's the weirdest, organicest stuff ya got?" Javier asked the tiny women tending the coffee bar.

She had a put-upon look that brightened when she saw his smile. And a cute face, framed by bangs where most of her reddish-auburn hair had been pulled back.

"How silly did you need to get?" she finally asked, cocking her head to one side just the perfect amount.

Lan. That was the nametag on her rather nice chest.

If you are going to stare at a woman's breasts, the least you can do it read and remember her name.

"Well, Lan, it's like this..." Javier began.

"No dark and stormy night interludes here, pal," she

interrupted him with a sharp laugh. "This is a coffee stand, not a poetry slam open mic night."

Javier laughed with her.

"I want something that started life in a bush, not a cracking tower," Javier said. "How can you serve my needs?"

"That's the problem with men," she said, mostly to herself, as she turned and bent at the waist to pull something from a bottom shelf. "Always thinking about themselves. Never focus on a woman's needs."

Javier was certain she would have had an easier time squatting, but then she might not have had a chance to show off her bottom at him. It was a nice bottom.

Somehow, the next button on her shirt had come undone in the process as well, so he was granted a nice view down her cleavage, as short as she was.

Afia-sized. Maybe a shade taller. Lighter complexion. Cute freckles. Bigger chest.

He wasn't monastically celibate. Behnam didn't require that of him when he was going to be away for at least a year and a half. But this woman was also a complete stranger, and Javier wasn't sure who the woman was a spy for.

Party like this, she was absolutely a spy.

He'd only been on planet three days now, meeting people and setting up more meetings with other people.

The life of a dilettante Ambassador-at-Large. Too much budget, not enough problems to solve, except what he invented lest he get bored.

At least he'd finally had a chance to meet the big players. The Governor of this dome was a faceless bureaucrat chosen to keep the peace by not siding with anyone and instead focusing on life support services and other technical mundanities.

But Javier had a cute redhead flirting with him. It was nice to know he hadn't reached that age where he was suddenly invisible to young women. Unless she was a plant. A honey trap designed to get him into some sort of incriminating situation from which someone might think they could blackmail him.

Oh, princesses of Ugen, *if you only knew the whole story.*

"And what might be a woman's needs?" Javier decided to play along. Just to keep in practice, if nothing else.

The women on the ship understood how to flirt. And that Javier would take *No* as an answer with no hard feelings.

Just for fun, he went ahead and ogled her chest again. Lan seemed to appreciate the effort on his part, as she did something he could only classify as a cleavage shimmy.

"The gold medal," Lan replied as she began sorting sleeves of something from a small tin.

"Gold?" Javier asked.

"That's where I get there first and you can come in second place," she grinned and licked her lips. "So I got a variety of loose leaf tea here from somewhere. What were your needs?"

Her wry grin and the way she licked her lips right then made most of the evening worth it. And the day of calls and messages as people decided that maybe they did want to meet with him after all, to discuss whatever scams and business they might have.

"Gimme," he said, holding out a hand.

She just passed the whole tin over and Javier settled it with the best way he knew.

Open a sleeve and take a sniff. Repeat until the receptors in the brain light up.

"This one," he said, handing it to her and putting the rest back.

"Man who knows what he's looking for," Lan noted.

"Discriminating palate," he offered ambiguously.

"I see." She started to work. "Patient enough to do tea right?"

"Time and attention to details," Javier said. "Great rewards available, if you aren't in a hurry to get there. Second place, as it were."

She put a bag into a mug and added hot water.

"You've got six minutes," Lan smiled ambiguously back at him. "How will you spend them?"

"Six minutes is barely foreplay when it comes to tea," Javier let his voice get quiet.

He noted the way her eyes paused to track the entire room behind him without pausing anywhere.

"And the various women you brought to the party?" she asked, suddenly a little more serious, without ever actually getting serious.

"Two of them are married to each other," Javier said. "One's still learning how to be a civilian and I'm her boss. Three of them have all made tea with me more than once. And the tall one's shot me, punched me, and given me four concussions in the last five years."

"You need an easier safe word," Lan chuckled. "So none of them warming your bed?"

"They're all playing second fiddle to the Khatum of *Altai*, and everyone's okay with that."

"Khatum of *Altai?*" Lan asked to Javier's nod. "Sounds powerful dangerous. Dragon lady. How'd you meet?"

"I broke into her starship and assassinated a man," Javier answered.

Nobody ever believed the story, assuming it was another tall tale.

Lan's face fell completely apart for a second before she recovered.

"Good one," she sputtered weakly. "How'd you really meet her?"

"Deadly serious," Javier said. "Someone with a lot of money wanted someone else done wrong and hired me. She appreciated that sort of thing."

Javier smiled at her, but felt the temperature drop precipitously between them as a rime frost suddenly coated the woman and she went white.

He'd have walked away at that moment. Come back in five minutes for his tea, but he wanted to make sure she didn't put anything in it when his back was turned. If he lost sight of it right now, he'd end up pouring it in a planter instead and hoping he didn't kill whatever bush in here drew the short straw.

Lan stepped to the far side of her little booth to put space between them, and Javier leaned back, turning enough away to indicate that he'd lost interest in case anyone was watching.

Someone always was. Usually either Sascha or Hajna, plus whoever else. Sykora still actively worshiped the Goddess of Death, so she probably had a plan to kill every single person in this room: individually, collectively, and probably alphabetically knowing her.

They waited in a hard, awkward silence. Javier nodded when the chime sounded. He lifted the bag and pressed it out by hand, chucking it into the trash so Lan didn't have to risk touching him.

Shame. Whoever had sent her should have warned Lan that there were likely to be some dangerous folks, even in a diplomatic sort of party as this.

Someone had screwed up, but Javier wasn't sure who.

He was dead certain, however, from others like her that he had known over the years that the woman was a cop.

PART TWO

THE RECEPTION WAS NOT close to done, but Javier was. Out of spoons. He had a pocket full of cards and promises of a dozen meetings with various players over the next two weeks to discuss business. Right now, he needed downtime.

He caught Sykora's eye across the room and nodded. She literally walked away from someone in the middle of a conversation, but he supposed she thought he looked more serious than he was.

Was he?

They had a weird relationship, he and the Dragoon, now that they didn't have to kill each other. But underneath it all, he was still pretending to be a different form of Navarre here, and she was still Hadiiye, even though Wilhelmina Teague had originated the role.

Him the principal. Her the bodyguard.

Sascha and Hajna perked up, but Javier shook his head at both. Afia was nerding out with someone and Bethany was listening to someone else in a bad suit pontificate. They were all big girls who could take care of themselves.

He headed for the exit and let Sykora's long legs catch her up.

Her face was a complicated swirl of questions, but he shook his head again, ever so slightly, so she subsided as they got into a lift, rode up three levels to the tower where the locals had ensconced a visiting Ambassador, and they walked along the hallway to his suite.

Just inside the door a small sphere rested on a table like a piece of abstract modern art. About thirty centimeters across, with a single eyeball lens in the front and a set of running lights around the bottom.

"Probe. Access Command Mode," Javier said as he closed the door. "Room security status?"

The lights came on and the thing lifted itself off its charging ring a handspan.

"Perimeter secured," Suvi's voice answered. "No rogue transmissions detected that fit any known surveillance frequencies. Were you expecting Bigfoot to make an assassination attempt?"

"Very funny," Javier answered.

He fixed himself a highball glass of whiskey and nodded Sykora onto the couch.

It wasn't actually Suvi in there, but a tiny shard of her personality downloaded from the ship. They communicated on an encrypted channel regularly enough, but the local version lacked most of what made Suvi *Suvi*.

Except her snark. That probably took up most of the memory.

"So I got propositioned in a variety of ways tonight," Javier began.

"Me, too," Sykora laughed. "Of course, in my case, they were just after my body."

"Very funny, woman," Javier sighed and took a sip. "The woman working at the coffee bar is an undercover cop."

That got her to sit up straight. The probe sphere stopped circling and centered its eye on him as well.

"How do you know?" Sykora asked, suddenly changing over into Hadiiye the killer, rather than just Djamila Sykora, the dangerous Dragoon.

Javier wasn't sure which one he liked more for this situation.

Both were in the top five deadliest creatures he'd ever met. You never knew when that sort of thing might be relevant.

"I've been arrested enough times," Javier replied, only partly a joke.

If you have never woken up from a three-day bender in a different county, wearing someone else's pants, with a Shore Patrol helmet on your head, were you even trying?

Javier didn't get that reckless anymore. Suvi's fault. And Behnam's.

And even Djamila Sykora, since he had spent several years trying to ambush the woman and make it look like an accident, same as she had been doing to him.

"Scenario impacts?" Sykora shifted gears and went utterly tactical on him now.

Javier shrugged.

"As far as you and Zakhar have told me, we aren't doing anything illegal on this run, right?" He had to ask, just in case.

"That is correct," she clarified, still seated but poised now, with those impossible legs pulled back, ready to spring her in any direction at a moment's notice.

She wasn't dressed slinky or anything. Dark blue pants, shirt, pale azure overshirt, but the woman was still 2.1 meters of honed killing machine with a brunette semi-mohawk. Still, men and women had been around her all night, talking, chatting, possibly attempting seductions.

How many of them had been cops?

"Are there even police worth mentioning around here?" Djamila asked after a second. "I got the impression from the party that the two big families controlled the system, at least at an economic level, which has always been sufficient in most places."

Javier stopped and stared at the woman for a long moment. Like so many others, he occasionally got distracted by the hard body and cute freckles and forgot what a first rate mind was hidden in there.

"Fritz mentioned both *Da Xing* and *Arsinoe* as interesting customers," Javier said. "You and Zakhar got any enemies left in those places?"

"Probably, but you'd have to ask him that," Djamila replied, glancing occasionally at the door to the suite, but relaxing.

Suvi had a moose-thumping pulsar in that sphere of hers, and enough local personality to know when to use it, even if the girl herself was up in orbit with a significant light speed lag going.

"Plus, Lan was working undercover, so they're here after someone else. I think, however, that she would have been better prepared if I was the target," Javier said.

"Give me the conversation again," Sykora ordered, so Javier did.

He didn't have a perfect memory or anything, but was able to give her a rough blow by blow account.

"Would she figure out that you used to be Navarre?" Sykora asked with a slight grin. "Perhaps you should stop trying to impress strange women in bars?"

"Pretty sure that's genetically encoded in me, lady," Javier groused at her. "But I'll see what I can do. You let your two know to keep closer watch and I'll talk to the others when I have time."

"Bodyguard mode again?" Sykora stood up now and towered over him from way too close inside his personal space.

Javier considered talking to the space between her breasts. It wasn't that far below his nose, or that far away, but she was just being her.

He could deal with it.

"Not as hard as that, but maybe a little sharper, yeah," Javier decided.

"What happens if the police come to you for help?" she asked with a sly grin.

"We'll burn that bridge when we get there."

PART THREE

THE SHUTTLE WAS MOVING SLOWLY to dock at Bamanie's wing of the orbital station, but there was time yet. They would spend a long afternoon touring a facility, followed by another private dinner and public reception.

Djamila supposed that she shouldn't be enjoying Javier's discomfort as much as she was, but there was no getting around that.

She'd been a soldier since she was ten, either training to be one, executing, or trying to find herself again when they were done with her at *Neu Berne*. As such, she'd never been at the center of attention, except when it was her team of killers preparing for a mission.

This was Javier's team. She wasn't offended that it was an all-female team that an outsider might mistake for a harem. He had that looseness around all the women here, even the ones that considered the touch of a male icky.

That was just Javier being himself.

But now he had a ring of sycophants around that. Middle-tier players who appeared to have been hired solely to fawn over the foreign ambassador and play to his ego.

Javier would probably let it go to his head eventually, except that Djamila and Afia would pop such pomposity before it inflated too far.

As they approached the dock, she looked over at Sascha. Djamila and Sascha had a bet going as to whether that cop would somehow have managed to get herself assigned to this catering crew. Javier hadn't complained about her after that first party, so nobody would have a reason to blackball her.

Djamila wanted a chance to see her in action. To watch her hands and eyes and determine just how dangerous this Lan woman might be.

At least Javier and his little circle were over there, being noisy and cracking jokes. Djamila was close to the main hatch.

She turned to Bethany Durbin, the Ship's Historian Javier had tracked down and recruited to help train Suvi and the rest of the crew what the far side of the galaxy might be like.

"Quick briefing?" she asked.

Durbin put away her tablet and looked up like a briefing officer with a captive admiral as an audience.

Ground Forces Commander, perhaps.

"*Da Xing*," Djamila said. "Current economic and military trends."

Durbin sat for a moment and considered her words. Djamila waited.

"*The Great War* saw *Neu Berne*, *Balustrade*, and the *Union of Man* largely reduced to second tier-states," the woman said after a moment. "The *Concord* remained untouched and traded with all players relatively equally. They assumed hegemony over a significant slice of the galaxy as a result."

Djamila nodded. Her childhood had been one of deprivation, even two generations removed from the peace treaty that ended *Neu Berne*'s imperial dreams on a flaming trash heap.

"*Da Xing* could best be described as an isolated remnant of a Pocket Empire, dating back to the time of Rama Treadwell," Durbin continued. "Over the last generation, they have been expanding by aggressively soliciting trade and military partners across their regional sectors. At the same time, the *Concord* has pulled back significantly, cutting taxes and military spending. Think of one tide coming in as another one recedes."

"You find merit in Aritza's expectation of a coming storm?" Djamila asked.

She'd heard the tale from the man several times. Fall of Rome or Fall of any of the Chinese dynasties. End of *Pax Britannica* or *Pax Americana*. The Terran League coming apart.

Human history was replete with examples, even before you got out of the home system in the Great Exploring or the Leap Outward. Corporate Wars, Resource Wars, or the latest Imperial stupidities.

"History supports his theories," Durbin shrugged. "A declining power and a rising power must both adjust their behavior, if wide-scale war is to be avoided. It has happened, but few enough times to actually merit mentioning."

"So *Da Xing*?" Djamila asked, bringing things back full circle.

"A war involving them and the *Concord* has some repercussions on *Altai*, but not much, considering the vast distance involved, and the expectation of a military front on the far side of the *Concord* from you. Us. The Khatum."

It was obvious that Durban still wasn't sure she would accept *Altai* citizenship, but Djamila didn't say anything. At some point, Bethany Durbin would have to choose, if only because she would be facing guilt by association.

Would Durban seek to return to active duty service if war returned? None of the others were likely to seek out war, but Bethany was young enough. Djamila would have to have a conversation with her at some point.

"So we expect *Ugen* to export materials to *Da Xing*?" Djamila asked.

She'd read the reports Javier had caused to come into existence. All of them.

"They do now, so I presume you mean an extension and expansion of such trade," Durbin corrected her. "Yes, that would follow the trend. Could the woman Javier met have been a spy instead of a cop?"

That latter in a whisper.

"Too soon to say," Djamila murmured back. "Hopefully,

nobody takes us seriously as a threat and we can just be peaceful merchants."

"And if not?"

"That's why we brought *Excalibur*, Durbin."

PART FOUR

Afia liked to remind people that she was an engineer, but usually left out the combat certifications bit. The guy she was talking to wasn't cute enough that she'd have a reason to explain the scar on her stomach where she'd nearly died at *Nidavellir* when a chunk of her escape pod had gone all the way through her armored suit.

Lucky for her that Ilan Yu had turned into a competent tech, or she would have just bled out before the Dragoon came along to save her.

Her stomach hurt today, but that was just the muscles reminding her when they made the transition between gravity wells from the shuttle to the station. It would be better in a few hours, after she got some food in her.

And he wasn't that cute. Probably an industrial spy, so she took his card and filed it in a pocket with the others she'd accumulated as she made her way to the bar for more brandy. The staff circling with trays had bubbly or simple wine. Not for her tonight.

She caught a glimpse of a figure coming up beside her and looked up. Everyone in here was taller than her, but that was Afia's lot in life. And everybody was a meter fifty tall when you got them into bed. Or something like that.

"Javier tells me you're his technical expert," a rich voice

seemed to quietly boom at her from a distance just a shade too close to be companionable, but far enough away that she wasn't calculating soft spots in his anatomy.

Afia paused and turned to study him. Fritz Bamanie. Their host today.

Nice enough guy. Older than her dad, but he probably didn't need to hear that. Still pretty well assembled, but not the kind of face that grew rugged and handsome as he aged. More like lined and hard.

"I have served with Captain Sokolov for eight years as a ship's tech," Afia smiled vaguely up at the man, wondering why he'd decided to stalk her.

Unless he was one of those men who were just constitutionally set on seducing every woman they encountered. Unlike Javier, most didn't take rejection well.

"What did you think of the greenhouse?" he asked.

She'd seen him talking to Javier and Rainier, so they'd most likely covered the organic bits. If he was asking as a tech, he wanted the metal covered.

"Above average for some of the stations I've been on," Afia smiled to take the sting out of her words. "Second quintile, perhaps. We've got a much better one aboard *Excalibur*, for all the obvious reasons."

"If you had the budget, what would you change?" Bamanie asked now.

From the tone of his voice, this was a serious inquiry, rather than a sneering counter-attack.

You never knew with rich people.

"Pocket mangrove swamp," Afia let her eyes smile while keeping her face studiously neutral. "Probably improve your filtration rates by about ten to fifteen percent, and lets you introduce several more species of smaller fish to keep bugs down. I'd add a jungle-style compartment to the temperate one you have now, just to expand the number of species of trees you can grow. Since you have smelters handy, a competent organic chemist can keep the fertilizer levels correct."

"You've done this before," Bamanie accused her.

She didn't know how much the man knew about everybody's past, so she had to keep things vague.

"I've been part of the tech team helping Javier with his botany station for about five years now," Afia said. "We can't get to *Terra* to get him another fifty cubic meters of Ukrainian soil, so we've had to adapt it to more local biomes."

"Ever tire of the diplomatic life?" the man asked in a roundabout proposition that had nothing to do with sex.

Probably.

"You couldn't afford me," she grinned. "I earn an officer's share plus corporate profits. My cousin runs the French restaurant on Deck Six and I get to see the galaxy."

"You have a French restaurant on a starship?" he seemed simultaneously intrigued and appalled, as any good gastronomer would be until they got deep enough into the details.

"*Le Bistro Parisien*," Afia laughed. "Long story. You should talk to Javier about it sometime."

"I will," he said. "And I will find time to bring you and my life support team together to talk about ways I could improve the system."

"Gonna be big," Afia warned him. "Like add another bay outside number two and build it out before you reroute water lines. Easier than trying to rearrange things."

"Indeed," the man bowed.

He grinned and slipped back into the crowd. Afia had a bubble of space around her still, where folks had pulled away from the two of them, and used it to get to the bar quickly.

Was everyone going face some sort of seduction attempt along the way?

PART FIVE

BETHANY HAD SLIPPED AWAY from the party. She wasn't going to anyplace in particular, so much as getting away from the noise and people. Most of them had been well-behaved enough to stop bothering her when she walked away from them.

Better than some of the *Concord* Navy events she had gone to, back when she still expected to have a career.

But she needed space. Quiet. A semi-dark place where she could sit for a while and recharge her batteries. If there'd been a library handy, she would have snuck entirely off, just so she could have overdosed on the smell of old paper or print laminate. Scents embedded in her lizard brain as home.

They probably had one on the station. The place was huge. Monstrous. Scale like *Concord* builders would have put up over a planet with fifty times the population. Granted, most of it was industrial, rather than mercantile or commercial, but big.

What it didn't have was signs, and she had not connected her handheld to the station's network. Something about information security and unsafe sex with unknown and possibly *Sentient* systems, although she wasn't sure if they had that much computing power. The *Concord* had been big on defending yourself against that sort of thing, and librarians were trebly so.

So Bethany found herself in a little nook, outside the party via the door closest to the kitchen where folks were delivering things to the party down the corridor. She'd turned the lights off when she found this space and climbed into one of the two chairs tucked all the way at the back like an appendix. From where she sat, eyes closed and heart slowing, she was in darkness, sucking it into her soul like the opposite of a rose.

Voices broke her concentration intruding. Whispers, really.

Bethany wanted to turn around and tell them to piss off and leave her alone when she caught the name **Navarre** murmured a little too loud.

She froze.

In her mind, she visualized this little pocket realm she had entered, Alice-like-entering-Wonderland. Main corridor, except even it was more of a side corridor. A service vein off that feeding blood and oxygen to the body of the station, but not the pretty parts where she had first entered.

Two and a half meter wide side corridor that dead ended about five meters back with a Missouri breakfast nook of bench wrapped all the way around. Minus the table, but she supposed that one could be added easy enough to give the kitchen crew a place to sit and eat without being out in the main room.

Two overstuffed wingback chairs facing each other in the center, except that she'd adjusted hers a little to face away from the light in the main corridor, casting her deeper into darkness.

Bethany assumed that the top of her head would be visible above the chair if she moved, so she pretended to be playing that children's game where you were safe as a statue and could only be hit if you moved.

"So that ship is *Hammerfield?*" a male voice asked, reminding her that the first voice had been a woman's.

"There are not that many old Galleons in service now," the woman replied. "Certainly not armed ones, and *Excalibur* most certainly is from the scans."

"Pirates?" the man asked. "Law enforcement?"

"He claimed that he'd been an assassin at one point," she said. "Navarre is a most notorious killer in certain sectors. Big enough that his legend has made it this far."

Bethany struggled to hear more. She wanted to turn her head to see who it might be, because they seemed to be standing right behind her, as though they had ducked out of the main corridor and not looked too closely at the darkness behind them before they spoke.

But if she moved, someone would see her. Recognize her. Possibly threaten her.

She didn't have a stunner on her. Why would she need such a thing around the Dragoon and her Pathfinders?

Bethany swore to never leave her room again unarmed. That had been the lesson for an out of work librarian, following a treasure map all the way to *Jackson Crossing*, well away and outside the *Concord*.

"I will bow to your experience," the man retorted sourly. "Have you a plan?"

"Not yet," the woman said. "My superiors are being notified and will address the situation. Nothing I was tasked with envisioned something like this."

"Very well," the man said definitively. "We will speak again. Now, I must get back."

Silence.

Not even footsteps walking away.

Bethany wondered if she'd been spotted, and was about to be attacked. Her heart certainly thought so, and she wondered if the two strangers could hear it banging loudly against the inside of her chest.

She counted to one hundred. Again. A third time.

Silence.

She turned her head like molasses dripping.

The hallway was empty. She noted the door to the kitchen was directly across from her, and closed. That was why she'd chosen this place. The staff would be too busy to take a long break.

Dare she wander accidentally into the kitchen and see if anything stood out?

No, best to return to the party and warn the Dragoon. Javier would have his hands full with other things, and the three women were along as bodyguards of a sort anyway.

Bethany just didn't know what kind of threat they might be facing.

PART SIX

JAVIER REMAINED SEATED. That way he wouldn't be tempted to jump up and yell at someone. Any of them.

All of them.

Sykora was standing in the middle of things, like she did. He was about eyeball level with her belt buckle this way, studying the *Neu Berne* Assault Commando logo rather than scowl and snarl back at her.

Sascha and Hajna had her wings, like they were supposed to.

Both Drs. St. Kitts were off to one side, watching but seated far enough away to be witnesses rather than participants. Afia was on Sykora's other side, standing but back a little.

Bethany Durbin was ramrod straight at attention, but Javier assumed that she was just falling back on training, rather than making a complicated socio-political statement.

Presumably. Hard to tell with that one.

"Okay, I admit it," Javier finally replied when he realized that they were all waiting for him to speak. "I screwed up trying to impress a pretty girl. But that's water under the bridge at this point and getting pissy about it isn't going to change anything."

He did scowl now, left to right.

"Bethany, at ease and sit your ass down in a chair," Javier ordered the young woman. "I'm getting a headache just watching you. The rest of you sit down, too. We need to approach this like civilians, not pirates, in spite of your natural inclinations."

That got a little bit of a laugh. Nobody ever set out to be a pirate. At least none of these people. Rainier and Emma weren't even close, being hired academics. Bethany had it in her, once she decided to stop being an unbloomed rose.

The other four all had warrants out for their executions somewhere.

As did he, but under the name Navarre.

And yeah, he'd screwed up.

Lesson learned: Don't try to impress pretty girls by being a badass pirate, unless you're in the kind of bar where a good night means nobody gets stabbed.

He'd forgotten that part, with Navarre too close to the surface.

Javier wondered if he needed to track 'Mina down so she could invent for him a whole 'nother identity into which he might squirrel. Nerdy botanist was too close to the real him and he wasn't comfortable being that guy around strangers.

At least not yet.

"Bethany, did you get a good enough read on the voices to identify them later?" Javier asked as folks dragged chairs around and stopped looming over him like an angry forest.

"Maybe," she said as she finally unbent and actually sat, instead of perching like a prized bird. "Her more than him, as she was speaking louder for the most part. Maybe facing me."

Javier turned to Sykora and extended his scowl. She was immune, but she always was.

"Can you help her surreptitiously record some of the big players we encounter and see if any ring bells?" he asked, recanting some of his anger.

Or redirecting at himself, which was where it should be anyway.

His fuckup. He needed to own it. If these people thought he was a pirate scouting them for an upcoming raid, he'd literally come all this distance for nothing. Maybe even made things worse.

But then, who could have guessed that Navarre would reach this far? Or the legend of *Hammerfield*?

"Can do," Sykora replied gravely, letting him wallow without so much as an *I told you so* to frost it.

"Also, nobody wander off by yourself, okay?" Javier said. "In spite of good things. Have a buddy in case somebody decides they want to get pointed with questions. That includes you two, Drs. St. Kitts. Sorry about that, by the way."

Rainier's eyes were a little big, but Emma just shrugged.

"We were aware of the company we would be keeping," Emma said with a frosty smile that warmed after a moment.

Javier actually felt the blush hit. Run all the way to the tips of his ears. The women around him all grinned at that, like they were in on the joke.

They might be. He didn't have many secrets from this group.

"If we've burned Bamanie as a contact, hopefully his rivalry with Luo is enough to keep us in business," Javier continued. "I'm still not ready to do deals to haul cargo, because I don't know what our next stop is yet. Bethany, you find a library and see who might be interesting around here to visit next. Take either Sascha or Hajna when you go. What am I missing?"

"Are we being too paranoid?" Bethany asked. "Spooking at shadows?"

Javier chuckled with the rest.

"Kid, there ain't no such thing in this business," he replied.

"No such thing as *too* paranoid?" she gasped.

"No such thing."

GENDARME

PART ONE

BETHANY WONDERED how Sascha and Hajna determined who would accompany her. It hadn't been even/odd. More likely the randomness of whoever felt like going to the library today.

They had started out in the station library today, three days after the party where Bethany'd managed to rile everything up. Or heard too much. Or maybe Javier had riled them all up. Something. She didn't have the right vocabulary to describe it.

But the library hadn't contained the information she wanted. Or rather, didn't have it in a format she wanted to deal with.

Seriously, who stored data in microbooks? That was like the most complicated method you could come up with, if you locked six engineers in a room and challenged them to get *obscure*.

Rather than trying to decipher it, she'd gone to the main mercantile arcade.

She had a palm stunner tucked into her pocket, rather than in the messenger bag she carried everywhere. Sascha had something similar, except that the other woman was apparently carrying three, plus a shock rod tucked into her belt behind the buckle.

Not playing around, as the pathfinder had explained it when Bethany had asked.

The station ran in tune with the planet below, specifically the main dome that it geo-synched, so right now it was rather early morning for doing business. Still munching donuts and sipping coffee kind of weather, even on a station surrounded by steel walls.

She didn't know what she was looking for, but Bethany was a librarian. The fleet had honed her ability to do research for admirals and captains who didn't know what *they* wanted, and expected her to find it for them anyway.

So she walked, a mug of adulterated coffee in one hand with a sippy cup lid keeping it warm. It wouldn't be on the main facing of the extended courtyard, the place that reminded her of nothing so much as a large intestine with the way it belled out into small courts between fire and vacuum break walls that were all open now.

No, it would be down in the small intestine, if you could describe a station that way.

"You got any warrants out?" Sascha leaned close and murmured.

The crowds were still sparse, but they weren't alone.

"Nobody has mentioned any," Bethany replied. "Until I met you folk, I had never left the *Concord*. Why?"

"Couple of gendarmes following us around," her dangerous bodyguard whispered with a grin. "Trying to decide if they want to arrest us or hit on us."

Oh. The thought of police had caused her to freeze up for a moment, but when she glanced that way it was a pair of young men in uniform, meandering around the courtyard.

The taller one smiled at her. Bethany blushed as she smiled back.

It had caused her to break her stride, not that she'd been walking fast, but Bethany found herself turned sideways and staring down what would be an alley if she was on a planet. Narrow and a little twisty, with signs stuck out from above doors, advertising things.

"Feel like being mugged in a dark alley?" Bethany asked Sascha with a sly grin.

"I thought you'd never ask," the woman chuckled.

She turned and headed down there, wondering if this was the entry to the small intestine, or maybe Wonderland. Certainly, the shops were small and tended to be darker. More for locals than tourists, if there was such a thing.

Noodle shop. Bar that consisted of four stools permanently attached to the deck and a counter, with the barkeep on the other side serving.

There.

News Emporium.

It took Bethany a moment to translate the ancient term but then she stepped into the space.

Her most recent apartment had contained a closet larger than this, and it didn't have an ancient woman seated behind a narrow counter, eyes watching her like a hawk. Bethany studied the walls.

After a moment, she realized that the images she was looking at were book covers. Each was about the size of her palm, pasted to the walls in a pattern she couldn't identify, unless it was by color.

She turned to the old woman, trying to find the words.

"Tourist or merchant?" the old woman suddenly asked, bright eyes studying her.

Bethany wasn't in uniform. Those had been left in long-term storage back home, possibly never to be worn again. At the same time, she was comfortable in greens, so pants, shirt, and shell were all shades of the color, from the depth of the forest up to new grass.

"Historian," Bethany finally replied after a moment to consider what the woman meant.

"Histories of *Ugen* there," the crone said.

Bethany shook her head. She glanced back to see that Sascha was still in the narrow corridor outside, and appeared to be flirting with the two gendarmes who had wandered along with them.

"I'm looking for context," Bethany tried to explain. "Old

newspapers charting the daily news of the planet for a long stretch of time."

"Why?" the woman asked crossly.

"Histories always get edited in the second draft," she replied. "The little details get stripped because everybody already knows them. Someone like me comes along later and misses things. I want to understand *Ugen*, not just read about it."

The crone studied her for several long seconds. Bethany wondered if the woman would throw her out now.

"How far back?" she asked instead.

"How far can you go?" Bethany countered. "I have a budget from the captain to add to the ship's library, and don't figure this will be our last trip to this system."

Actually, it probably was. Right now, Captain Sokolov and Suvi were probably keeping a running calculation of what they would need to do to rescue the team and shoot their way out if trouble came, but Bethany didn't need to tell an old woman that.

"Got a reader?" the merchant asked, pointing at a line of such devices on the shelf behind her.

"Nope," Bethany said. "Didn't even know what format it might take."

"Microbook," the woman smiled evilly. "Everything on *Ugen* uses microbook."

Of course it did. At least she wasn't lying about having a budget and cash on her to get something.

Suvi thought at around 30,000 times the speed of a human on her current hardware. Afia or someone would have to modify a reader so she could control it, but Bethany didn't figure it would take the woman long to process everything after that.

She studied the boxes on the shelf. Translated the prices, balking a little at even the cheapest one. Tapped the middle one. It had some features that looked useful, without being forged in pure platinum and rhodium-plated afterwards.

"*Ugen* News Star," the woman said, pulling a box from a pile near her feet and opening it. "Complete set. Seven hundred years."

"People actually want that sort of thing?" Bethany asked, shocked. "Enough that you carry it?"

"Secondhand," the crone grinned now like a night monster spying an unlocked door. "Owner died of old age. Estate sold me all his books cheap."

She quoted a price for the whole. Bethany wanted to stomp out, but saw the smile in her eyes.

Time to dicker.

Eventually, she made it out of the shop with enough cash left that she could buy lunch and maybe have coffee, too. Or talk Sascha into treating her.

Those two cops happened to be standing close when she emerged, nearly running into the one talking to Sascha and possibly hitting on her.

"What'd you find?" the pathfinder asked as Bethany stepped close, the woman shifting around so that the four of them, including those two cops, didn't quite fill the corridor if someone wanted by.

Rather than explain, Bethany pulled it out of the bag and handed the box to the woman.

"Seriously, you're weird," Sascha said with a grin.

"Hey, it's why Javier hired me, you know," Bethany grinned back.

"News?" the taller, cuter cop asked.

"I'm a historian by training," Bethany said. "Ain't no jobs back home when they start cutting budgets. I managed to score this one. My job is to understand local cultures for the bosses and keep them from accidentally insulting our hosts or something."

"Seven hundred years of news?" the man asked.

"You know a better way to understand you folks?" Bethany asked back archly.

"Maybe," the man retorted with a grin. "But it probably involves buying you drinks."

"I can get awfully nerdy," Bethany warned him with a smile. "And it's way too early for drinks. What time do you guys get off duty?"

Both cops blinked a little. Like maybe girls were supposed to be demure and shy or something.

Y'all never met *Concord* Naval Officers, have you?

But she didn't say that. Just smiled at them. Marked down the time and got an address in the main courtyard for an early lunch.

The boys went back to the main intestine, but Bethany wanted to explore Wonderland deeper.

"So, what do you think?" Bethany asked Sascha when they were alone again.

"If the short one wants to frisk me for national secrets, I might just be willing to play along," Sascha laughed. "But if those two were spies, they're not doing a particularly good job about it. Still, I'll let the Dragoon know. Presumably, she'll want to join us for lunch, or at least keep watch from close."

"You think those boys are a threat?" Bethany asked.

"Only if you still happened to be a virgin, Bee," Sascha laughed. "So why did you get so much news?"

"It will give Suvi something to do," she replied. "Nobody ever goes back and excises the incriminating details from stuff like that, so you get a much balder look at how people think by what gets reported."

"Oh, that's a good thing to know," Sascha said. "Should we maybe bail on lunch?"

"No, I want to see if the authorities are serious about things."

"And if they are?"

"Sokolov's always close."

PART TWO

"You're sure?" Zakhar asked Suvi in the privacy of his office.

"Aye, sir," his favorite Yeoman answered. "The station does not have a *Sentience* aboard. Nor do any of the systems or vessels currently broadcasting."

"So you are the only one in system?" he pressed.

"Affirmative," Suvi nodded. "Why is it important?"

"You forget how rare your kind are, Suvi," Zakhar explained. "The *Concord* is one of the few places that could afford to build you. The *Union* and *Neu Berne* could build versions once, but only at their peak, which is long-since past. For *Neu Berne*, perhaps this vessel was the last. They might have the technological sophistication now, but not the economic might."

"Understood, sir," Suvi replied as what sounded like a placeholder.

"You're also a warship, Yeoman," Zakhar let his voice grow firm.

It was like dealing with a young Yeoman, even as he was feeling like an old fart today. He would be sixty next year. Suvi, might be one hundred and twenty-something, but she'd only been a First-Rate Galleon recently. Before that, a simple probe-cutter.

In her mind, she was still occasionally just a kid, fresh out of training.

"I doubt that there's anything even remotely equivalent to a Class II Warmaster anywhere nearby," Zakhar continued. "And it would take a Class III, or equivalent force, to take you in combat. Of course you make them nervous."

"Oh," Suvi said simply.

That one syllable, but she was working at a speed that blinded organics.

"But we're not pirates," Suvi said, probably just to reassure herself. "Do we invite some of the locals aboard to inspect the crew? Set their minds to right?"

Zakhar caught himself before speaking. That wasn't an entirely bad idea. A true pirate ship would have several times the crew he had. His was roughly triple what he would need if this galleon were merely a cargo hauler, because he was also doing science and exploration along the way as well.

"I'll talk to Javier and Djamila when they call," Zakhar said. "For now, you keep up your defensive analysis of the system and make sure nobody can sneak up on you. If they try, I am ordering you to immediately take all defensive measures you deem necessary before consulting an organic."

"Defensive?" Suvi asked, clarifying.

No *Sentience* was ever supposed to open fire on a ship manned by humans without first receiving direct orders. That was supposedly coded directly into their personality chips when they were first impressed.

However, and Zakhar had had a long conversation with Javier on this very topic, the Science Officer had gone in and reprogrammed her at several points. One of them was to let her operate all the guns as she saw fit, rather than relying on orders from Javier. Or Zakhar, now, since it was his ship Suvi flew.

"Defensive only," Zakhar replied. "Get away from them first. I promise you that anyone gunning for us or Javier is going to get stomped like an empty can of tuna. Walvisbaai should have learned their lesson. Others should have drawn the same conclusions. If they are coming, they mean us harm, but you're my ace in the hole."

"Aye aye, sir." She brightened. "Other orders?"

"Set up an encrypted channel, next time one of the two of them call," Zakhar ordered. "Wake me and make sure Piet is on the line as well. We might need to plan for warfare."

"Even though we come in peace," she said, not bothering to frame it as a question.

"We come in trade, Suvi," Zakhar replied. "They decide on the peace part."

PART THREE

"WHAT DO WE KNOW?" the man asked, his face scrambled on the screen and his voice run through a modulator to obscure anything someone might intercept. For Lan, it was always better to think of him merely as "The Man" so that she wouldn't ever accidentally use his name and blow his cover as her contact.

She had learned enough signals encryption to understand that the trade craft she was using was sufficient against the locals, but that was a First Rate Galleon in near orbit. A warship powered by a *Sentience*, no less.

It might even be the fabled *Lost Flagship* of *Neu Berne*, but she needed to hear from her superiors for confirmation. *Ugen* was simply too remote a world: socially, geographically, even intellectually.

If it wasn't so important to so many players, she would have never ended up here. But too many economies relied directly on exports from *Ugen*. Too many spies.

Too many criminals.

"We have kept them under watch while they have been aboard the station," Lan replied, brushing her bangs back out of her eyes and wondering what she looked like and sounded like at the other end of the channel. That scrambling went both ways. "However, nothing that they have done has raised any hackles or threats as yet. Agents have kept them under routine surveillance and even contacted them socially."

"Should you contact the man again?" the man asked. "Break your cover as you did with me?"

Lan blushed.

She shouldn't have reacted as she did at that party, but the pirate had caught her off guard, so brazenly admitting his crimes, even so far from any system likely to have jurisdiction.

But at the same time, a man like that couldn't be a smuggler, could he? Smugglers were supposed to maintain a low profile. Not arrive with supposed Ambassadorial credentials, even from someplace as far away as the semi-mythical *Altai*, clear across the galaxy. That felt almost more like something a con man would do.

They had broken off short of doing anything, but she suspected that the man knew more about her than he had let on.

"I will make that determination when the courier arrives with updated information," Lan said. "For now, my suggestion to you would be to treat the man as a business rival. My superiors are aware that you have been working with us on this case and continue to be at great pains to make sure that your organization is not caught out as things progress. Thank you for your assistance, in case I have not said it enough times before now. We would not be this close to taking down your enemies without it."

The man grunted and cut the line rather than replying with some flippancy she might have expected. Lan cut the line as well and leaned back in her chair.

Her apartment was spare and sparsely decorated. But it was more of a hotel room than anything, a pre-furnished space she had a six month lease on, as though she was merely a lower-middle-class worker in the food services industry of *Ugen*.

As covers went, it allowed her to attend such parties as the wealthy elite held regularly, without requiring her to maintain a more significant cover identity.

And even her contact here, the man on the line, didn't truly understand her purpose. He was merely using her to help destroy his principal rival, and do so in such a way that he retained white hands.

Nobody wanted to admit to the things they did to get ahead in business. Not even the *Union of Man*, who had sent her to *Ugen* with a cover as a law enforcement agent looking to investigate and destroy a ring of smugglers working in tandem with *Arsinoe* to flood the market with the sorts of hard-to-fabricate metals that made warships cheap to manufacture and repair.

The last thing the galaxy needed was another war, but everything Lan had seen pointed that way. Soon, too.

Right now, piracy was almost out of hand in enough sectors that trade was at risk of being disrupted.

What would an Ambassador from *Altai* do to that? If he was on the level, could he help break some of the piracy problems? That vessel was more than enough to take on anything, if it was what the whispers suggested.

Why did an Ambassador need a battleship?

But Lan supposed that a smart one would travel in that sort of style if he wanted to be protected. She wasn't sure that the *Union of Man* had a single warship capable of being a threat to a ship like that.

They had, once, but that had been before her parents were even born. Back at the end of the Great War, when the *Union* and *Balustrade*, with assistance from the *Concord*, had finally broken *Neu Berne* for good.

But the cost had been prohibitive. The cheap loans that the *Concord* had advanced, to buy the war materials necessary, were only now finally starting to be paid off. Worlds had drifted or broken forcibly away in the aftermath, until only the cores of the three nations were still intact.

And like the *Concord* of old, *Ugen* would sell anything to anyone who met their price. At least some of these folks.

Lan looked around her office. Bland water colors that came with the suite. Industrial resin furniture with a faux-laminate designed to look like wood. Taupe carpet under her feet designed to outlast generations of people.

Nothing here that suggested any clue about her past, present, or even future.

The Ambassador had wanted to flirt with her. Had.

She had broken off on him just at the moment when it might have gotten interesting, but she was a cop at heart, even as she was supposed to play the role of a spy.

But the man had been right.

She needed to talk to this Javier Aritza again.

And see if she needed to arrest him, destroy him, or simply ignore him.

It couldn't be accidental that he was here, could it?

PART FOUR

JAVIER HAD NEVER IMAGINED that *ennui* would be the natural outcome of these sorts of cocktail parties as a lifestyle. But then, he'd never been *important* before.

Behnam, the Khatum of *Altai* herself, didn't do things this way. Of course, she had a flying lake, a starship with a swimming pool in the middle that was two kilometers long and a kilometer wide at the middle of the oval.

She held luaus when she wanted something interesting. Or movie nights where people sat on inflatable floats while a vid was projected in the air.

Nothing diplomatic.

Javier looked around the latest round and sighed. At least the booze was good, but he didn't get blind, stinking drunk these days, either. Maybe two glasses of wine circulating. Later he'd have a couple fingers of the good whiskey, depending on the company.

But seriously, the languor around here was almost thick enough to stop a knife. It didn't help that he'd seen at least half of these people at the last four such events. Presumably, the other half were what made it worth investing in. Certainly, he had enough offers to haul cargo and a few high-end tourists willing to pay stupid rates to live for a time aboard a battleship born under an alien sun.

But he most obviously wasn't cut out for this ambassadorial life. Too much like being a grown-up.

He mingled. Offered witty commentary when necessary. Talked brass tacks with folks. Sipped bubbly that was truly extraordinary.

"Enjoying yourself, Javier?" Fritz said as he stepped out of the crowd.

It was notable how quickly a bubble of open space appeared around the two of them when the man did that.

Power, though not necessarily from fear. Respect for the amount of money and influence the man had, and presumably a willingness to use it enough to remind people, but not so much that folks started to take offense and do anything about it.

Rich people occasionally forgot that a man with nothing left to lose has nothing to stop him from doing rude shit.

Javier had never made it there, but he'd seen it. Usually outside the naval compound on the surface of a planet somewhere, where old sailors, long since broke, begged and busked for enough money to buy some food.

Javier kept his grimace, like his sigh, inside. In his parents time, the social services available for folks like that had been sufficient that nobody had to sleep rough.

But the storm was coming.

"Indubitably, sir," Javier nodded. "Contemplating the nature of cocktail parties."

"If there is a more useless way to spend time, I have yet to find it," Fritz nodded back. "Necessary as a social lubrication, but I'd rather be at a live musical event. Or hosting a smaller dinner for an intimate group of friends, where we could talk about outrageous things without risk of giving offense."

"Is that an invitation to sneak away from the party and commit juvenile hijinks?" Javier inquired with a gleam in his eyes. "Spray paint a mural somewhere or get chased off by Shore Patrol?"

"No, but there's no reason this event has to continue all night," Fritz countered. "Especially as you and your party will be trading my hospitality for Andak's tomorrow. What did you have in mind?"

"I don't know about *live* live music," Javier said. "But *Excalibur*'s pilot is a music nerd of the first order, as is the ship herself."

"The ship?" Fritz exclaimed.

"Suvi," Javier nodded. "She's not the original *Sentience-in-Residence*. That shit was from *Neu Berne*, but he died a long time ago."

"Fascinating," Fritz said. "There are rumors about your vessel, but obviously your crew had been very tight-lipped about things. How did you come to possess a First Rate Galleon?"

"That, my friend, is a story requiring more than just a glass of wine, and probably far fewer witnesses willing to testify later," Javier chuckled. "Why don't you make arrangements and I'll have a shuttle swing over in a while to haul a small party aboard so we can maybe have a more personal chat."

"Yes," Fritz said, coming to a sudden conclusion. "You do that. I think myself and a plus one, if that's acceptable?"

"Capital," Javier said. "We'll probably need a couple of hours at my end, depending on sleep cycles."

"Until then." And Fritz vanished back into the crowd.

Javier located Sykora towering over the crowd and made his way towards her. She met him halfway.

"What evil things are you up to now?" she asked in a bright voice so at odds with all his memories of the woman.

"Hauling Fritz aboard *Excalibur* to talk turkey," Javier said. "Can you wake Del up and have him fly the assault shuttle over in an hour or so?"

"Who's coming?" she asked, transforming before his eyes into that damnable Goddess of Death persona she adopted when it came time to kill people.

"Fritz and a date that I suspect isn't his spouse," Javier answered. "You, me, Del. Fritz would like some music, so it gives Piet and Suvi a chance to shine, and Zakhar an opportunity to weigh the man's soul with that captain thing he does so well."

"What about the others?" she asked, establishing targeting vectors or something as she looked over people's heads.

"We'll let them know we're sneaking away from the party, and to behave themselves," Javier decided. "If this was bigger, I'd bring Rainier and Emma along, but I get the feeling Bamanie wants something deeper than a trade exclusive. The women can all take care of themselves for a day. It's not like we're going far, and we have a Galleon and your gun bunnies if someone gets mouthy."

"Is this wise?" she asked.

"Everything up until now has probably been for show," Javier said up to her. "Now he wants to know about me, us, and the mission."

"What are you going to tell him?" Sykora leaned down to talk quietly.

"The worst thing possible," Javier grinned. "The truth."

PART FIVE

Lan didn't like it, but the man had been insistent. Demanding in ways he never had before.

She had exactly two choices right now. Join him and walk right into a pirate's den, or burn Bamanie as a contact permanently and potentially watch her whole case implode.

Rich, powerful men don't like being told *No*.

Lan smiled and pressed the button to open the hatch, holding her breath.

It opened onto a passenger waiting area looking through a clear window into an internal landing bay. There was a monstrous shuttle over there, shutting down as the outer bay doors closed. Lights started to flash, warning of pressurization.

But Lan was looking elsewhere already. Three people had turned when she entered the lounge.

She made her feet carry her into the room, unaccustomed to such recalcitrance. She was a cop. Why was it so hard?

Lan knew the answer, though. Too many years undercover, where any mistake, any publicity was a bad thing. A deadly thing, frequently.

She would be outed now, no two ways about it. But Bamanie had insisted.

Demanded.

Normally, Lan would have dressed in black today. Subtle

colors designed to blend in at an event, where everyone else was sparkling. An undercover cop had to have an understanding of fashion, because everyone expressed so much of their subconscious personality that way, and Lan had to remain in someone else's character all the time.

Frequently as the help, and not a player.

Here, she had stepped it up a little. Blue sun dress with black leggings and a floral print on both in white. Pockets, but they were empty, with pouches on a leather belt holding things Lan had brought with her, few though they were.

Quiet and feminine. Absolutely not a cop, but she doubted anybody would be fooled into expecting her to be Bamanie's groupie or date.

He was there, watching her with triumph in his eyes. Bamanie was dressed in a muted business suit, a brown so dark it might be bronze. Lan wondered what game the man had won by exerting control over her now. She'd been driving before.

The Ambassador raised an eyebrow as she approached but remained perfectly silent, just watching her. There was no smile, but no scowl either. He wasn't dressed as severe, with flowing pants and a top like a half-kimono over a nice shirt, everything in shades of blue that actually matched up with her own rather nicely.

The scowl was on the tall woman. Lan didn't even come up to her shoulders and almost felt like a child around her. Brown hair cut spacesuit short on top and buzzed on the sides, like a form of mohawk. She had earrings and studs on both sides, but nothing through her nose or anywhere else. Freckles.

Dressed in an outfit that somehow quietly screamed ex-military without ever one thing saying how Lan knew it. Pants in a tougher material than the men. Buttoned up jacket with a belt. Epaulets on the shoulders. All of it in a gray a shade darker than dove.

Bright, green eyes like a predator staring down at her.

"Interesting," was all the tall woman said, but she still moved in such a way that the amazon was standing behind Lan on a flank as she approached the two men.

Bamanie turned to the Ambassador.

"Javier, I believe you might have encountered Lan Cornish at one of the parties we've attended this week," the man said with a cruel streak to his voice.

"Charmed," the Ambassador replied, nodding but keeping his distance.

Silence. Not even small talk.

Lan felt like the ultimate outsider, back to her early days of trying to build up a network of informants when she first made detective a decade ago. Before her superiors decided to make her something of a spy.

Cop, but spy. Never forget that you have a badge, buried in a bank box in case of emergency.

Not that it might do much good with this crowd.

"Djamila Sykora," the tall woman said abruptly.

Lan turned and got to shake the woman's hand, feeling even rougher cal.uses than her own.

"Lan Cornish," she replied automatically.

The silence stretched. Lan felt like a show pony, but didn't have enough understanding of the power politics at play here to step right.

And there was a lot of power politics suddenly swirling around her, like a tide threatening to knock her over and drag her out to sea to drown.

"Del's ready," the Ambassador announced abruptly, keying open the inner hatch to the landing bay and striding away as soon as the door cleared.

Fritz Bamanie followed with a sardonic smile for her as he left.

Lan stood there for a moment, wondering if this was the point where someone put concrete shoes on her and tossed her off a pier.

"After you," the tall woman, Sykora, gestured politely, so Lan followed the two men, glancing back once because for all her height the woman made no sound whatsoever on the metal deck plates.

She had been expecting a personnel shuttle, based on

Bamanie's explanation. One of those could have fit in the landing bay of the monster she was looking at. The two men walked up a landing ramp wide enough for assault vehicles and deep enough for maybe four of them.

Lan followed, feeling the first hint of nerves.

Deep space was almost as good a place to dispose of a body as underwater. Maybe more so, when you could let a corpsicle burn up on re-entry.

She had a stunner in a pouch, but from the way the woman behind her moved, it was clear she'd never get to it in time. And drawing it now would be a bad idea.

Better to play dumb and hope. She'd left messages behind, so someone might be able to find out what had happened, if she didn't return in the morning to disarm the send function.

The inside of the shuttle was rough. Old. Beaten.

The Ambassador led them through a hatch and suddenly they were in a nice lounge like the one on the station. Fold-down chairs in leather with harnesses for maneuvering, arranged in rows on the left and a bowl on the right.

They ended up seated in something of a circle. Lan found herself across from the Ambassador as she hooked everything and watched the other three carefully.

"Del, we're good," the man suddenly said to the air. "Back us out."

Lan felt the ship shimmy once and then lift ever so slightly. The landing bay must have already been emptied as soon as the tall woman came aboard and closed the ramp, because they were out of gravity range and floating within seconds.

"Okay, we're in deep space now," the Ambassador announced, like he'd been waiting all this time, as he turned his attention to Bamanie but gestured a hand at her. "I'm not kink-shaming, but is there a particular reason you decided to bring a cop?"

PART SIX

JAVIER WATCHED THE WOMAN FLINCH. Not much, but you didn't need much. Only a cop would have reacted that way. Innocent civilian would have been confused first, then probably indignant after a heartbeat.

But he really didn't care about her. She was just a victim here, near as he could tell. Fritz was up to something. Probably no good, since he'd wanted to get this cop into a compromising situation away from witnesses.

Was he thinking he could hire Navarre to kill a gendarme? Was anybody really that stupid? Trick question. He could still make a living playing poker on a station somewhere if he got bored or Behnam threw him out.

"I'm interested in how you knew she was a police officer," Fritz smiled and purred.

Not why Javier had called her one, but that everyone here seemed to know what she was.

Rather than answer, Javier reached out and keyed the intercom.

"Del, you got anybody feeling frisky on your scanners?" he asked simply.

"Should I?" the old man in the Hawaiian shirt answered from his flight deck that still looked like a *Merankorr* brothel.

"Doubtful but the probability is higher than zero," Javier said, closing the circuit.

That would light a small fire under Del's ass, in an old *Balustrade* Assault Shuttle that had been significantly upgraded in the last year. Even Javier's old probe-cutter *Mielikki* would be hard pressed to be a threat to Del right now.

Red lights came on everywhere as Del's paranoia ignited.

"Was that necessary?" Sykora asked simply, aware of what Del would be like now.

He turned to Fritz and smiled.

"Was it?" Javier asked the man point blank.

"No," Fritz let his face grow serious now, like maybe the practical joke had gone a little too far and everybody needed to dial things back some before crazed ex-pirates got *frisky*. "How did you know?"

"Cops give off a scent," Javier said in a harder voice, turning to watch the woman now. "I've been arrested too many times to miss it."

She stared back at him with a stern look. At least she wasn't going to deny it or get weird. Not that anybody would successfully start something Sykora couldn't finish, mind you.

Maybe Lan Cornish understood that already.

"Are you really an assassin?" Cornish asked him abruptly. "They tend to be far more serious."

"You ain't seen serious, lady," Javier growled at her. "But the man I assassinated is still around."

"How is that possible?" Cornish snapped.

"I destroyed all his identity papers," Javier said. "The secret ones that showed him to be the missing Jianwen Emperor who had been overthrown by a bunch of bureaucrats and industrialists. Without those, there was no more Jianwen Royal family. No heir. Didn't need to harm a hair on his head after that, so as far as I know he's still out there living under an assumed name."

Javier liked the way her mouth puckered in distaste. He didn't bother explaining that someone had hired Navarre expecting a *Mass Casualty Incident* splattered all over the decks of Behnam's yacht. None of this cop's business.

None of anybody's business.

"So you really are Navarre?" the cop asked.

"Nobody is Navarre," Sykora spoke up before he could flay some skin off the woman. "That is a character in a book used to frighten people."

"And the events at *Nidavellir*?" Cornish pressed, maybe pushing her luck, but Javier let the two women talk while he watched Fritz out of the corner of his eyes.

This was still Bamanie's ambush. What did he want out of it?

"A pirate altercation that left the galaxy a better place," Sykora summed up an afternoon of death and destruction at the far end of several weeks of planning and execution.

Dead station, shattered and de-orbited expertly by a pretty good snooker player with a big enough hammer.

"Additionally, you have no jurisdiction, whoever it is you work for, Cornish," Sykora leaned forward enough to threaten the woman.

Cornish didn't argue. Smart move on her part. *Nidavellir* was wholly owned by Walvisbaai Industrial, until then the most notorious of the so-called pirate clans plaguing *Concord* space and other neighbors.

Good riddance, as far as Javier was concerned.

"So what's your connection, Fritz?" Javier derailed the confrontation before it got out of hand.

"Detective Cornish is blackmailing me to help her with an investigation into Andak's activities," Fritz said with an off-handed nonchalance that told Javier just how well the woman must have his balls in a vice.

"And?" Javier turned to Cornish.

Smart woman shrugged rather than arguing.

"Someone is going down for it," Cornish said in a professional voice. "Bamanie chose to help us, so that we can make an example of Luo instead."

"Rough game, lady," Javier told her, impressed that she could bluff those stakes.

This was an expensive place to play such games.

"Who do you work for?" Sykora asked now, shifting back to Bad Cop.

As if she ever stopped playing that role.

Cornish hesitated.

"The *Union of Man*," Fritz spoke up in her place, drawing a daggers stare from her.

Javier turned to Sykora.

"You got any outstanding *Union* warrants?" he asked offhand.

"Probably," Sykora shrugged in turn. "Jane Doe Number One, most likely."

"You admit to being criminals?" Cornish asked, shocked.

"We've gone straight now, lady," Javier ground on her verbally. "The *Concord* doesn't like me one bit for what I did to Walvisbaai. Haven't been in *Union* space in years. I'm a legitimate citizen of *Altai* now, an accredited Ambassador, and traveling science nerd. We're looking for honest trade and cultural connections with one of the most interesting planets I could find, and then we're going onward for other things later. You got a problem with that?"

Still, he watched Fritz, wondering why the man had outed a cop in such a nasty way.

What was his game?

"Don't get involved with any smugglers while you're here," Cornish managed.

Javier had been better threatened by three-week-old kittens, but he was willing to score her one for brass.

"I'm not headed back to *Altai* for a while," Javier replied. "So if someone approaches me about hauling a cargo somewhere around here, you might have a problem, but it will be a legitimate cargo, FOB *Ugen*."

She subsided.

Once you got past the cop bits, the woman was still cute, verging on beautiful. He'd treat her as Fritz's plus one for now, unless Sykora found a need to bounce the woman off a bulkhead later.

Djamila Sykora was an expert at that sort of thing. Javier felt safe.

"Landing in three minutes," Del announced over the comm. "All hands return to your seats and bring your tray tables to their upright and locked positions."

Javier grinned. He'd never met a crazier pilot in his life than Delridge Smith.

Nobody got gray hair flying assault shuttles into combat, but Del had. Still would, if it became necessary again.

But Javier's problems weren't with anybody outside the shuttle right now.

PART SEVEN

Suvi understood from the body language of the four people emerging from Del's assault shuttle that something had gone wrong. Not bad wrong, but sideways in directions none of them had expected.

The Dragoon wasn't holding a beam weapon on the two newcomers. Neither of them were acting aggressive. Javier had that *whatever* thing going that told Suvi he was a crocodile down in the weeds, waiting for lunch to arrive.

She opened a shard channel to Zakhar's station on the bridge. She could be in dozens of places at once with this hardware. A little old by modern standards, but still way more awesome than her birthship had been.

"Something's not right," she said simply, displaying a feed from the landing bay and highlighting the way people walked.

The Captain watched for an eternity of three seconds while she contemplated redecorating her personal quarters with a new paint job or something.

"Agreed," Zakhar said after that. "Let Djamila's people know to step up their game a notch."

"Is violence necessary?" she asked.

"Violence is rarely necessary, Yeoman," the Captain retorted with just an edge of gruffness to his voice. "But if you are prepared to unleash the hounds of hell on someone at the drop of a hat, they usually decide to behave themselves."

"Oh."

She'd spent too much time in service. Or alone with Javier and the various generations of chickens. Sometimes she forgot that she was a badass warship with a pirate crew these days.

She reached out a spare tentacle and moved the alert setting on the Gun Bunnies up a level. Not to *Start shooting immediately*, but maybe to *Be armed and not taking a shower*.

On a screen, she watched Iqbal and Demyan yell at the other four and start organizing their break room. Guns would come out and be checked.

Anybody threatening Javier and Djamila would have to go through her, anyway, but she'd let the others have a pound of flesh if it became relevant.

"Piet ready?" Zakhar asked, breaking her back into the current tense on his station with her primary shard.

"Affirmative, sir," Suvi replied. "Not sure I understand the situation, but we're there."

"Too many cocktail parties in public," Zakhar said. "Think of it as a private reception with exotic music."

"As you say, sir," Suvi acknowledged.

She flitted back to the landing bay, after double-checking the forward lounge where Piet was.

She wasn't fooled by the way Fritz Bamanie had an unknown woman on his elbow as an escort. The body language was all wrong, like she was a hostage or something.

Javier hadn't had anything bad to say about the man, but Suvi wondered about that. And why they had brought everyone aboard like this? If it wasn't a party, should there be guns?

Granted, the Dragoon could handle any three random strangers, but still, there was principle involved.

Javier brought them out of the landing bay and into the main corridor now, through various airlocks and such. Into an elevator, so she finally had everyone where she could scan them with enough horsepower.

Bamanie was feeling triumphant, from his heart rate and

smile. At what, she had no idea. Javier was relaxed. The Dragoon was keyed up for violence.

The woman was nervous. Heart rate elevated. Perspiration in spite of temperature. Pupils dilated a little too much when Suvi looked her right in the eyes.

Something's not right here.

But Javier knew Suvi was here, and hadn't said or done anything, so she played it cool.

Piet had the room set up as a salon for intellectuals. He always claimed that being able to stretch out on a couch was just as important to the listening as pacing was for others.

Not having a human body, she couldn't tell one way or the other.

Still, they were getting close now, so she invested her primary awareness shard into Piet's salon and watched.

Suvi usually thought of Piet as her musical partner in crime. Javier had taught her to love music and even compose it, but he didn't like noise all that much.

Piet Alferdinck might look like a quiet music nerd, average height and blondish hair he kept short, but the man secretly composed symphonies when nobody was looking. Pretty good ones, but she understood that all musical taste was relative.

Technically sound, comparing it favorably to the grand, choral pieces that had been popular in the 66th Century and the early Pocket Empires Era.

She personally preferred the 63rd Century, but Suvi was a sucker for DeManx's Symphony #43. Or Kwellon and her stripped-down symphonies designed to be played by no more than sixteen instruments.

"Fritz Bamanie, allow me to introduce you to *Excalibur's* Pilot, Piet Alferdinck," Javier said as everyone got into the room. "Lan Cornish, Piet Alferdinck."

Hands got shaken. The woman was calming down now, like she'd been expecting something much worse.

Suvi put a feed from the room down to the Gun Bunny break room so they could follow along and know what they might be facing.

"Fritz and Lan, this is my best friend in the galaxy, and my second favorite goofball," Javier said as he turned to a screen where Suvi was watching.

Suvi considered blushing, but settled for a smile. She and Behnam completed different parts of Javier Aritza, and Suvi had come to appreciate what that other woman could do for him. And they were best friends. Behnam was just his lover.

"Suvi was my *Sentience* aboard the probe-cutter *Mielikki*," Javier continued. "We were able to install her here later, and she is the First Rate Galleon *Excalibur*. She and Piet also compose music."

Gasps, but that was always the case. Humans who composed were rare enough. She wasn't aware of any of her cousins that had ever been given enough freedom to try.

All Javier's fault, yer honor. I was just an innocent schoolgirl when he did his dastardly deeds on me. And if you'll believe that, I got a planet to sell you in Iogen Sector.

She appeared in her standard *Concord* Yeoman knockoff uniform and smiled.

Bamanie was all cagey with his emotions, but probably assumed that a suave face was sufficient and that she wasn't scanning his silly ass with every system in the room. Sucker.

Lan Cornish was relaxing more. Not calm, but she'd separated herself from Bamanie and stood closer to Javier and Piet now, with the Dragoon keeping everyone in line.

"Wetbar with whatever your needs are," Javier announced and pointed. "Piet's in charge of music. Suvi, could you ask Captain Sokolov to join us?"

"Sure," she said.

The Captain was already in motion, but he understood how to make an entrance. After *Nidavellir*, a lot of people understood that about the man now.

Zakhar arrived and got introduced around, with Mary-Elizabeth now technically in charge on the bridge.

Suvi watched people fix juice, wine, and stuff. Javier stretched out in a comfy chair. The Dragoon surprised her and Javier by doing the same. Zakhar took a chaise lounge. Bamanie claimed one end of the couch, eyeing Cornish like he was daring her to sit close to him.

Suvi was developing a dislike for the man.

Cornish surprised them by perching on the arm of Javier's seat like they were on a date. Certainly, his body language shifted into flirt mode.

"Piet, what have you got for us tonight?" Javier asked.

"One of my own," Piet replied in that quiet voice that made you lean in to listen.

Or turn up the gain on your various microphones, but Suvi already knew that was coming.

"Do tell."

"Suvi, could you play selection one, please," Piet leaned back and looked at her screen. "This is 'Spring Rains and Summer Heat' from my fourteenth symphony."

"Fourteenth?" Bamanie asked, shock finally letting some emotion break through that smooth exterior.

"Correct, sir," Piet grinned. "I have completed twenty-three at this point."

"Impressive."

Suvi let the music rise at this point and conversation ceased for a time.

It was instructive, listening to heart rates as the music played, but she and Piet might have planned it that way and not told anybody.

Both strangers freaked right out at her piano concerto for six hands in A#, but liked it after they got into it. She didn't tell them she'd spun up an four extra arms to play it. Humans didn't appreciate that sort of thing.

The three hours passed with a few intermissions. It seemed to do whatever it was Javier was up to, because she caught him dozing a time or two.

Eventually, the time passed and Javier escorted the two strangers to the flight bay, sending them home with vague promises to chat later about cargo hauling jobs, once something was over.

Whatever it was that was being underplayed and underhanded.

She watched Javier return and look at the immediate group in the lounge. Her, Zakhar, Javier, Piet, and the Dragoon.

"Good enough," he announced. "Shit's gone weird."

PART EIGHT

ZAKHAR WAS NOT surprised by the rapidity with which Javier shifted mental gears. He'd had five years now to watch the man put on one mask after another, code-switching as the situation evolved.

"Here or bridge?" Zakhar asked.

"Here's fine," his Science Officer said. "Bamanie and Luo don't like each other. Cornish is a cop working on some sort of undercover case to take Luo down, and using Bamanie to get there. We've made nice with the one guy. Tomorrow, we're supposed to drop back down to the planet and spend a few days with Luo before opening bidding to haul some cargo or passengers around. Thoughts?"

"Bamanie does not like Cornish one bit," Piet spoke up. "Bad body language there."

"Agreed," Javier said. "Beyond her being a cop and him probably in up to his eyeballs in things that might be extraditable, anything specific?"

"No, but she'd rather flirt uncomfortably with you than sit next to him," Sykora spoke up. "She probably would have preferred you invite her to stay the night, just so she wasn't alone with him on the shuttle ride back."

"Maybe next time," Javier looked at her, bemused at the suggestion.

"Is Luo a threat?" Suvi asked. "From what Bethany has assembled, he seems to have the smaller organization. More focused on mining and undersea stuff while Bamanie owns orbital space."

"The two seem to tolerate each other," Javier noted. "But I've only ever seen them in public, playing nice. I'm hoping that we've charmed the man enough that he wants to hire us later."

"Be safe then," Zakhar got earnest now. "You'll go from instantly in communication and under my guns to someplace where we can't talk to you. Can't easily rescue you if you get into trouble. Del will enjoy himself, though."

"Noted, but it's not in anyone's interest for something bad to happen to me down there," Javier said.

Zakhar hoped not but wondered if Javier had gotten in over his head?

SUB-MARINER

PART ONE

JAVIER KNEW that submarines as a technology predated even powered flight, but it was still cool to be riding in one. Doubly so a fancy yacht like this one. Same same as being in space, but totally different.

Like the one he'd first landed on when he got to *Ugen*, this vessel was long and rounded on the edges, like a finger with a flat top you could walk on, but missing that enormous flight deck for landing shuttles. On a calm day, enough of the ship could surface that you could walk the deck, but usually the conning tower was the only part that would emerge, like a weird aquatic monster.

Because the yacht was something of a long-range cruiser, every cabin had portholes with light rings around them so you could see outside. Or trick sea creatures into coming over to explore. As a first class passenger, he had a fantastic view.

To top it all, according to the brochure on his bed when he arrived, the bow compartment on the top level was wrapped entirely around transparently, so you could sit up there and see the sights, or chat with other guests.

Yeah, Luo was going all in to impress the Ambassador from *Altai*. How many people had a *spare yacht submarine* lying around that they could just bring into service to tour? Apparently, the man's main yacht was even more sumptuous, but was designed to cruise with a total of two couples as passengers and twenty crew.

His eight would have been pushing things a little.

So they were in the backup yacht. Javier just loved the sound of that, and considered seeing if he could talk Behnam into something similar, just for the phrase.

Backup yacht.

Javier had gotten everything into his cabin, but he'd unpack later. They had returned to the briny depths of *Ugen* after departing from the main dome, and were headed roughly north now, cruising slowly at a depth of about one hundred meters.

Ugen had originally been seeded with *Earth* species by one of the standard oceanic packages, back in the early days of terraforming. The shapes he'd seen out his window were all familiar, but he had to stop and appreciate that the thing the length of his arm, swimming outside his window right now had adapted from a bioluminescent whaleshark.

Lights on the side of the ship were apparently a mating call kind of thing, because there was one out there right now answering as the ship slowly puttered along.

At least he hoped it was nothing but a whaleshark, and not something bigger, meaner, and maybe hungry.

You never knew in the depths of an alien ocean.

He killed the light and decided to head forward. A little coffee and some mild socializing might be fine. It had been mid-morning when they loaded up and headed out. Not quite lunch, but that wasn't far off.

But first, an Arnold Palmer to drink.

Long, skinny ship. Central corridor on each deck. Three decks, with passengers on one, support staff on two, and engines and stowage all the way at the bottom.

Bethany was just emerging from her cabin as he came even, so they ended up walking together.

"Learned anything interesting?" Javier asked breezily.

"The galaxy is weirder than even you," she fired back with just the perfect amount of droll sarcasm.

Javier grinned.

"Kid, you ain't seen nothing yet," he replied.

"That's what frightens me."

He understood now why his old professor, Dorn Hetzel, had recommended the woman. She fit right in with the rest of his crazies, even down to the ability to imply a double eye-roll across a room without once moving or speaking.

So his humor was at the peak when he opened the forward hatch and let himself into the main salon. Sykora was there already. She toasted him with a mug of coffee as she grinned.

He turned to locate the barista and felt his stomach clench.

Bethany bumped into him from behind when he stopped walking, then apologized and slid around.

Javier gritted his teeth and swallowed the profanity before it emerged. Instead, he walked over to the coffee bar and smiled at Lan, working behind it in the same black outfit she'd been wearing the first time he saw her, down to the extra button undone to show off a little more cleavage than was professional.

"Coffee, tea, or me?" she asked in a quiet voice with a snarky smile.

Javier glanced back to catch all of Sykora's smirk. Afia had her nose against the glass, but paused to grin at him. Bethany looked a little confused, then she saw the situation and apparently suppressed a snort from the way her shoulders flexed and her face went perfectly blank.

"Coffee," Javier replied after a long beat, catching Lan's smile that answered the others. "For now. Espresso with two shots and some caramel and chocolate syrup. Real cream. Hot. I have questions, but I'm not sure if pillow talk is safer or not. How did you get here?"

"I'm on Luo's staff," Lan replied innocently, her hands already in motion so fast that Javier had a hard time keeping up. "That first party you went to was one he hosted."

"Oh," Javier nodded. "So I might have met you, but don't know any of your dark secrets?"

"Just like in the real world, Ambassador," her smile got a little frowny. Serious-like. "But it is a small boat. I'm sure I'll run into you from time to time."

"Indubitably," he said, taking the cup from her hands just like that and auto-piloting over to where Sykora sat. Bethany was close. Afia wandered over.

Sascha and Hanja entered and did just enough of a double-take that Javier noticed, and then went and ordered something anyway.

"I feel like perhaps we are lacking actionable intelligence on the situation," Javier said quietly to the tall woman.

"You should probably brace our host for details, then," she replied, smiling. "Unless you think I might get more out of him."

He hated it when she smiled like that. No good ever came of it.

And while women like Djamila Sykora were frequently a man's fantasy, few men actually liked it once they got there.

Greener grass, and all that.

"Maybe she'll whisper sweet nothings in your ear as she frisks you," Afia added innocently. "Known a few guys got off on that sort of fantasy."

"Not funny," Javier replied. "She's looking for a reason to arrest me anyway. I don't want to have to have Suvi break me out of jail. She'd lack subtlety."

Blinks and white faces at the consideration of a First Rate Galleon who was angry.

Some of them had seen the aftermath of *Nidavellir*, when Suvi was just being professional. And *Excalibur* had been through a full refit and restoration since then.

Class III Warmasters would have to be polite to her now.

Javier started to say something else when the aft hatch opened and Andak Luo entered. Gone were the fancy duds, swapped for white slacks and a simple pullover shirt with a standing collar and a logo over the left breast.

The man smiled and nodded, got a glass of red wine, and moved this way, shooing Afia back into her chair when she made to stand and give way.

Instead, he pulled up one of the wooden chairs with a hard

bottom. Made him stand out a little with all the plushness the rest of the team had selected.

"Welcome to *my* domain," he gestured grandly out the front glass and smiled at them. "I appreciate that you've been with Fritz all week and no doubt seen his impressive facilities, but I have something he's never managed to match."

"What's that?" Javier decided he could play the straight man here.

"An entire alien world," Luo beamed. "Four thousand years of evolution playing out around us, in a world where humans have not strip mined things with giant nets. New species of whales and other creatures have started to emerge. All manner of nautilus variants have niched themselves in. I'm just sorry that you and Dr. St. Kitts are botanists and not zoologists, because there are some amazing creatures down here and I can't really get anyone to study them at a professional level."

"You aren't spending enough," Javier suggested.

"Oh, we have a good university at the main dome, but all the kids with aquatic tendencies tend to study mining," Luo waved a hand negligently. "Useful, but *Ugen* is so much more than pretty beaches and ore haulers."

"What is it, then?" Sykora spoke up, leaning forward to draw the conversation her way. "All the tourism brochures work to emphasize those elements. Possibly to the detriment of others."

"We are an entire planet, Djamila," Luo focused on her now.

Using her first name surprised Javier. He hadn't been aware that she'd gone past formal with the man. Maybe he could sic her on him for more information?

"No planet is a monoculture, in spite of what you see in those silly action vids," the man continued. "There are no jungle worlds. No ice planets. The only place you get extremes is on an airless moon somewhere. Hell, we've got forests on the surface of some of the smaller continents, containing species no other planet in the galaxy has, but I'm not prepared to haul Javier and Dr. St. Kitts to them right now."

"Why not?" Sykora asked.

"Storm season in the southern hemisphere," Luo's face got serious. "The geography of this planet is especially nasty for typhoons and the places I'd send you are getting hit every seven to ten days. It's part of the reason we all live in domes below the ocean's surface. Just easier. In fact, we'll be traveling beneath at least two of them over the next few days, depending on how they track."

"Will we notice?" Javier asked.

He rarely did planets anymore. Space was easier and generally safer, because all the risks were calculated and mitigated in advance. Plus, in his various botanical stations, he could control the weather like some primitive's god.

Fulfilling to the ego, on a petite level.

"No," Luo turned back to him now. "Again, the depth of the ocean insulates us against almost everything."

"So why not floating platforms tethered to the domes?" Afia asked, going all nerdy. "Why submarine carriers for landing shuttles, where you then have to sail over to the dome?"

"The domes themselves are tough," Luo grinned at the pixie kodiak now. "But if something goes wrong, you end up with a big chunk of metal free-falling. Maybe a sharp corner fractures something, or even just weakens it. Then you maybe develop a leak or a soft point. Risk of rupture. In space, everyone jumps into a suit and that's that. Here, you have to be protected against enough pressure to squish you instantly."

"Yeah, but..." she began before subsiding. "Yeah, right. I could see that. Okay, flip the question. You've got mines going down into the ground. Why build domes on the ocean floor? Why not burrow down and then maybe go sideways with tunnels to connect all the domes with subways?"

Luo's face got utterly serious. The room seemed to get quiet.

"It wouldn't be any fun," he pronounced, holding the joke just the perfect beat before laughing out loud contagiously. "Seriously, we could do all that, but then you're underground and can't look up at a pod of whales swimming overhead. Couldn't sail along with glowsharks, cloak squids, and other weird things. The world is supposed to bring you joy, madame."

"Oh," was all Afia had to say.

The others caught the thread as well. This was a different man from the Andak Luo who had first hosted them, all stiff and formal. Maybe he'd begun to relax around them. Certainly, he was taking a week from his schedule to escort them around.

There would be blocks of time where the man would have virtual meetings, but he seemed to be looking at it as a vacation. Javier decided to join him in the fun.

"Will we do any diving?" he asked.

"We can," Luo nodded. "There's a four-person submersible pod aft that is equipped for light science, in that it has waldo arms and the ability to pick things up from the sea floor. Most of where we're going will be far too deep and too far from land for good swimming, but the return arc takes us along some of the greatest beaches in the galaxy, as far as I'm concerned."

"Awesome," Bethany chirped.

Javier did a double-take, but she seemed sincere. Maybe the bookworm was into beach weather. He'd have to remember to give her a week on *Shangdu*, Behnam's personal lake, when they got back. She'd been in the library pretty much since the day he hired her.

Useful, but he needed to remember that not everyone was as introverted as him and Piet when it came to people.

"Now, with that said, I mostly came to check that everyone was settled," Luo rose. "I have a call with some managers shortly, and then I'll meet everyone for lunch?"

"Looking forward to it, sir," Javier said.

"Please, call me Andak," the man said.

"Javier."

"Excellent," Andak smiled. "See you in a bit."

He was gone. The only stranger in earshot was Lan, but she was studiously playing her part, over behind the counter, so Javier smiled once at her and then kept his voice low.

"Updated thoughts?" Sykora asked.

"Convincing Behnam to endow a professorship at King's

College to study evolutionary oceanic biology," Javier retorted. "I forget that animals change over time, just like plants. Takes them longer, but as the brochures point out, this planet is four thousand years old with *Earth* species."

"How does that help?" Afia asked.

"Careful, squirt, or I'll convince her to make you a Professor of Mechanical Engineering tasked with building flying submarines," Javier grinned.

"Already got a few designs, pumpkin," Afia grinned back. "You let me know when you want to go into the ship-building business."

"Ha." Javier studied everyone around him. "So keep your noses clean, as far as the cops are concerned. Study the world we're sailing through, with an eye towards exportable exotics worth hauling maybe as far as *Altai*. When we get to the mine, maybe there's something there we can suggest to improve things. Otherwise, we steal as many ideas as we can to haul home for asteroid mining."

"Giant space dragons," Bethany said deadpan. "Sail up to a big rock and take a bite out of it, swallowing it down to a smelter and pooping bar stock."

"We already do that," Sykora said with a hint of disgust.

"Yeah, but they're ugly and functional," Bethany continued with a laugh. "I mean build one that looks and flies like a dragon. I've heard Javier's stories about the Land Leviathan. Why don't people dream that big most of the time?"

"It's expensive," Javier said.

"Javier, your fiancé, the Khatum has a starship built around an artificial lake larger than most orbital stations," Bethany got serious. "Afia, maybe you need to design a mechanical sea monster instead of just a submarine."

"Anybody ever done something like that?" Afia asked.

"Not that I'm familiar with, but I haven't looked, either," Bethany replied. "Guess what I'm going to be doing."

"As long as everyone remembers to enjoy themselves," Javier reminded them. "This is a mission, sure, but it's also a vacation on an exotic planet under an alien sun."

They accepted that good-naturedly and slowly drifted off with their own thoughts, mostly watching in silent awe as the yacht explored the oceans of *Ugen*.

Javier remembered Andak Luo's earlier comment about sheltering from storms under the oceans, instead of up on the surface. That had protected them for centuries, even as new overlords took over orbital space, time and again.

There was a bigger storm coming.

What could *Ugen*, and Andak Luo, teach them about surviving it?

PART TWO

BECAUSE NOBODY ELSE WOULD, Afia had taken it upon herself to publicly be nice to the cop lady, without blowing her cover in the process. They were in a confined space, after all. Lan was one of about thirty crew members, split about half and half between hotel staff and ship's crew; excluding this one woman, the rest were mostly invisible except for cleaning cabins and meals.

Javier didn't trust Lan yet enough to sneak off and fool around. Djamila and the Pathfinders tended to be a tight clique. Bethany liked to read. The doctors hung out together and did married folks kinds of things.

That left one nerdy engineer.

"So you're my primary barista?" Afia asked, looking around the empty lounge, just to be sure. "Like it?"

Ship's time was middle of the evening. If they were cruising on the surface, it would be close to sunset, from the way the west was brighter.

"Yup," Lan answered. "Pay's damned good. Food is provided from the same kitchen you eat at. Hours are ugly, but only because I have to be on call whenever guests need something. The crew eat out of a different kitchen. Mostly automated down on two. The boss has a personal steward and she's responsible for him while he's in meetings. I have him when he's entertaining you."

"So Javier's stupid early hours mess with your sleep cycle?" Afia asked.

That boy had been with his chickens too long. Got up frighteningly early, even when the birds weren't around. More than once, Afia had rolled over and gone back to sleep when he got in the shower and didn't roust herself until much later.

"A little," Lan agreed. "But nobody except you is up late, so I'd normally be sitting here reading for another hour, and then crawling into my bunk to crash for a few hours."

"You like the job?" Afia asked, wondering if there were microphones in here overhearing conversations.

She'd known a few people who used secret recording devices, and she'd never find them if they were hard-wired into the walls.

"Better than most of them I've had," Lan replied, not breaking cover.

Afia leaned forward, kind of over the counter like she might with a cute boy back home.

"So you're really one of *them*?" she whispered, without alluding to who *they* might be.

Lan shrugged.

"So what do you expect when we get to the mine?" Afia asked, voice quieter now. More intimate. "Anything good?"

"Doubtful," the woman shrugged again.

It helped that they were almost the same height. Less off-setting psychologically.

"Why's that?" Afia murmured as Lan leaned a little closer, too.

Girls sharing secrets, you know. Maybe talking about boys. Maybe going to steal a kiss. You never know, if anybody was watching the room on a security camera right now.

Afia listened in the silence for the whir of a camera lens zooming in. Javier had taught her a few things about sneaky, and Suvi had cameras and pickups everywhere that needed servicing regularly.

"In the vid show, there's always a smoking gun lying around in a file, just waiting for a cop to break in and find," Lan murmurred. "Never works that way in the real word. Most of the time I catch a name or a place someone happens to mention too loud and pass it along. Someone else adds it to a matrix and start drawing connections. Think thread connecting notecards tacked to a wall. Sometimes it's that primitive, too."

"And what's that do?" Afia asked, intrigued now.

She'd been a sailor, a pirate, and a union shop steward, in that order, but most of her adult life had involved sneaking around and specifically not talking to cops.

Even cute redheads.

"Somebody hears something," Lan continued. "Does something stupid. Then you figure out who to arrest quietly. Sweat them and offer a deal if they roll over on someone more important. Rinse, repeat as you get progressively more interesting and colorful characters."

"Risky?" Afia asked, still leaned a little too close.

Lan didn't seem to mind.

"Working without a net," Lan grinned just a little. "Nobody to call on as the cavalry, unless your boss decides to really be one of the good guys that steps up at the right moment."

"Javier's as good a man as you're likely to find," Afia said. "He took a bad situation and saved our asses so many times I've lost count at this point. Got a bunch of us rich enough that we could have probably retired a while ago, but I'm having too much damned fun."

"He's a killer," Lan said.

"You've heard about what went down at *Nidavellir*, right?" Afia asked, watching the other woman also not leaning back. Lan nodded carefully. "I was the one that triggered the scuttling charge on the ship that we slammed into that station. My first and so far only command, but Javier relied on me, because trust me those bastards deserved it."

"Hundreds died," Lan's voice got a little husky.

"Pirate base, lady," Afia snarled. "And it was only dozens.

Bad people. Assholes. Even at our worst, we were never like them."

"The rest of you were pirates?" Lan asked, eyes wide now.

"We captured Javier in the first place," Afia grimaced. "Cut up Suvi's ship but he hid her from us until he could turn the tables. Except instead of killing us, he recruited Sokolov to get revenge on even worse people. The rest of us probably deserve to hang for way more bad shit than Javier ever did."

"Why are you telling me this?" Lan asked, perhaps realizing they were almost nose to nose right now.

"Boss is trying to do the right thing, always," Afia said. "Brought the rest of us in from the cold when he didn't have to. Gave Wilhelmina Teague all his money, costing himself years of servitude. Made peace with the Khatum enough that they're a serious thing, as much as he might flirt and occasionally fool around. Won't mean anything other than the moment."

"And me?" Lan asked.

Afia considered her words carefully. Didn't want to give the wrong impression.

But what was the right impression?

"He thinks highly enough of you not to blow your cover, Lan," Afia said. "That makes you good people. Wondered how you might feel about fooling around a little here, completely in your cover, of course."

"Of course," Lan replied drolly, face on the verge of a sarcastic eyeroll that just made Afia smile more.

"Don't figure you'd get a chance to get off the boat and tour the mine," Afia continued. "Not as an employee. However…"

"I see." Lan's voice turned husky now. "I'm not supposed to fool around with guests, you know."

"Right, which is why you've got that third button always undone?" Afia grinned, pointedly glancing down the woman's front enough to maybe see her belly button.

Lan grinned back.

"Maybe," Lan answered with a saucy gleam in her eyes. "I'm just a poor innocent here, with orders from Luo to take care of his guests, after all."

"So if I wanted to drag you off somewhere for a hot and sweaty snog, and maybe bring you along in a few days when we toured an underground, undersea mine, I'm just taking advantage of your trusting nature?"

"Yer honor, she corrupted me," Lan giggled quietly.

Afia leaned that little extra bit and kissed her. Lan did not resist. Seemed even corruptible, but obviously it would take a lot more work to be sure.

"Let's go back to my cabin and play a game of good cop/bad cop," she whispered at the woman.

"I thought you'd never ask."

PART THREE

Djamila could not suppress a smile, even as she kept the snicker inside. Andak Luo had barely batted an eye when the *Union of Man* police officer showed up, obviously as Afia's plus one for the tour, holding hands and giggling together quietly.

Djamila didn't engage with females, but she'd also gone far too many years celibate around Zakhar, actually afraid to knock on his hatch and express herself. And now she had two men who loved her, one here and one waiting patiently back on *Altai*.

Afia was much more flexible, it seemed. Or an actress playing a role designed to stretch her some.

The best part was the eyeroll Javier had at the situation. Djamila. Hajna. Sascha. Rainier. Emma. Bethany. Afia. And now Lan.

Good thing the Science Officer had brought Andak Luo along, or it would begin to resemble a man with a harem. That might go to his head, except he'd been pretty celibate himself on this mission.

"I'm not sure why," Djamila caught Rainier talking to her wife just ahead. "I think I'd be better served had we stayed aboard the ship."

"I disagree, Rainier," Djamila spoke over the woman's

shoulder before Emma could reply. "You might be the second most important person present, after Javier."

"Why is that?" she asked as both Drs. St. Kitts paused and turned.

They were in the mine now. Not down in the working parts, but walking along a metal frame catwalk that connected offices and equipment designed to move rock around without human involvement.

Djamila gestured to their surroundings.

Raw stone, still showing marks from explosives drilled in to fracture the hard faces, as well as scratches left by the enormous rotary blades that drilled into the bedrock like a mole twenty meters in diameter.

"I see conduit for wire and fresh water pipes, Rainier," Djamila explained. "Lights regularly. But I do not see plants of any kind. Most ships and stations use a botanical element as an air purifier, but here they are scrubbing carbon dioxide and other traces from the air and cracking water for oxygen. Hydrocarbons are collected and bottled, but still represent a breathing risk."

Djamila watched the lightbulb come on in the woman's eyes. Emma was already there, and grinned silently as Rainier came around.

"So they should treat this like a station?" she asked with wonder, perhaps speaking more to herself than the others.

"The situation is not all that far removed," Djamila pointed out. "Sealed environment, surrounded by hostile and dangerous atmosphere. Limited space. This has been set for maximum efficiency, but I wonder what botany might do to improve things."

Rainier's eyes suddenly got serious. Professional. Possibly professional offended. She immediately stomped off after Javier and Luo at the head of the little column.

Emma paused long enough to nod and mouth *thank you* before striding off after her wife, Emma's long legs making it an easy chore.

Yes, Djamila had wondered why Javier had insisted on

Rainier St. Kitts initially. But the woman was probably more intelligent than Javier was, and the man was smart enough to admit it. Engineers always think they have the best solution, but forget that the other sciences can make useful contributions to health and quality of life.

Emma St. Kitts had Javier working out four days a week and in better shape now than he probably had been when he last wore a uniform over ten years ago.

Djamila nodded and strode off in pursuit of the party, a shepherd keeping a watch on her flock.

Wilhelmina Teague wasn't here to do it, but that woman had left her mark on all of them in her brief time aboard *Storm Gauntlet*.

Djamila Sykora could take up that mantle in her stead.

PART FOUR

Rainier didn't rush right up to the two men at the head of this little expedition, but she perhaps used the noise of her approach to communicate a level of pique as she walked.

Both men stopped and turned, faces expectant and eyes wide with curiosity.

Rainier paused, marshalling her thoughts as though this was a budget meeting planning for next school year's labs. Bureaucracy had always been her second most formidable talent behind guerilla gardening.

"Andak. Javier," she nodded politely to the men, mentally sharpening a pencil to do financial battle. "I am intrigued by the lack of potted flora at regular intervals. One would think an industrial facility of this scope and nature would be well served to make such a minor investment, especially in light of the obvious long term benefits to health and profitability."

She smiled at the men. Her mind always saw Captain Navarre when she first looked at him, just before Djamila Sykora and her team had rescued them from a second band of pirates on *Svalbard*.

But he really was Javier Aritza. She had learned not to play poker with the man, or the others.

The way his face went perfectly neutral right now reminded

her of how much money she had lost that first time. A most expensive lesson then, but still bearing fruit years later.

"I'm not sure I understand, Dr. St. Kitts," Andak replied now in a polite voice with sufficient confusion that the man was not placing an ambush in her path.

"Your mine has roughly seventy-five permanent employees on site, correct?" she asked, gesturing to the quiet woman who had been leading and pointing things out.

Rainier had lagged at the rear of the column, only in front of Djamila, and had not caught name of the woman giving the tour the first time. It seemed rude to ask right now, as she had stopped and seemed to be fading into the stonework at the moment.

"Correct," Andak agreed vaguely.

"On a space station, there would be significant numbers of potted plants, designed to help scrub the air naturally, thereby reducing the load on your life support facilities and extending maintenance cycles significantly," she noted.

At the University of Uelkal, back home, she had helped design such systems for a few private enterprises. It had helped bring in cashflow to an always-underfunded research department.

Andak Luo stared at her blankly. But he was just a rich investor, not a scientist. Still, she needed to speak up now, rather than just retiring to her botany station, as she might have.

"The act of blasting rock, of running machinery, of a dozen other myriad things, produces harmful, aerosolized chemicals," Rainier pressed on. "Your life support system must find them, scrub them, and then neutralize them. I'm presuming at significant cost, both in terms of hardware, but also wear and tear. Yes?"

"I would have to check the actual numbers, Dr. St. Kitts, but I am happy to assume that as a starting point," he replied, warming now as she got him onto running a successful business. "I presume you have improvements you might suggest?"

Javier had somehow slipped backwards almost a whole step

in the last few moments, until she found herself facing their host alone.

She quailed inwardly for a moment, but then Rainier decided to pretend that Andak Luo was a less oily version of her old boss, MacWilliam Harvison, the university's president. She could do this.

Then Emma stepped up on one side of her and Djamila on the other, and Rainier suddenly felt like a goddess facing the two men.

"Depending on your chemical outputs, it would be easy to identify which things to plant and in what quantities," Rainier smiled now. "Certainly ivy close to the working machinery, as a number of species will absorb all manner of nastiness and you can just trim the runners and leaves back regularly to compost or bury as needed. Other things will also clean the air, and a variety of them will provide fresh fruit along the way, potentially stretching your kitchen budget significantly while improving the nutrition of your staff."

The man seemed to stagger backwards mentally, even if he remained still.

He turned to Javier now, face questioning.

"There might have been a damned good reason I specifically recruited a botanist, Andak," Javier grinned slyly. "This one, in fact. And brought her down to the surface of *Ugen* with me, where the locals might be able to take advantage of her fresh eyes and outsider status to make suggestions someone else might have been ignored for. Especially considering her genius with plants."

Rainier gasped, but hopefully only in her head. She had convinced herself that Javier had hired her and Emma as something more of an apology for all the nastiness that had occurred at *Svalbard*.

She had not considered that the man was after her professional qualifications in his mad quest to do right in the galaxy.

She could do right as well. Make the galaxy a better place.

But you didn't make things better just at the macro level. It was also necessary to do the little things, like putting plants in a mine to help the miners live healthier lives.

That also worked.

"I see," Andak replied after a long moment no doubt spent juggling budgets and that natural inclination to not make any changes until things got so bad that heroic measures might be called for. "My apologies, Dr. St. Kitts. Would you be inclined to a consultancy while you are with us?"

Rainier felt a flush almost like an orgasm pass through her frame.

Then a second one as she considered her response. Hopefully, she wasn't glowing right now, but Javier smiled.

"Andak," she nodded in acknowledgment, including both men. "As my expenses and salary are already being covered by the expedition, a fee is unnecessary, but I would be happy to write up my notes into a series of workable suggestions if I could get a copy of your life support quarterly reports to draw in. Perhaps long term you might also look into adding a botanist to your staff for such things."

Andak had paled a little. It was strange being able to convince someone that easily. But MacWilliam was a hard-headed shit who could only be relied upon once you had his signature on the paper. Not until.

The man turned to their guide and Rainier finally got a look at her. The nametag on her chest said Roya, and she smiled carefully at them.

"Make sure to forward a copy to me as soon as you are in a position to, and I will make sure that Dr. St. Kitts receives it," he ordered Roya. "And make sure a half-day meeting gets added to my calendar in forty days to review implementation or rescale the budget appropriately."

"Understood, sir," Roya said.

"Rainier St. Kitts, I may have been remiss earlier," Andak continued. "This is Roya Andree, my lead geologist. Not the mine manager, but the person most likely to be able to implement your suggestions. Roya, Dr. Rainier St. Kitts and her wife, Dr. Emma St. Kitts."

Rainier shook hands with the woman, as did Emma.

"Thank you, Dr. St. Kitts," Roya said.

"My pleasure," Rainier said.

They got everything settled and began to tour again.

Rainier hadn't forgotten Javier's words. She had wondered, but she understood now.

She could make the galaxy a better place. He was giving her that opportunity, but he needed her input, her help to do it.

She smiled and took up a station behind the two men, deciding to pay better attention to the rest of the tour.

PART FIVE

JAVIER WATCHED the machine bore through the bedrock of *Ugen*, hollowing out a long tunnel and pushing ore back into carriers for other machines to haul away. He wasn't sitting in the command station, that was being run by a pair of geologist engineers who seemed to know what they were about. Instead, he had the front row standing space right behind them, with Afia and her girlfriend on one side and Andak on the other.

As things went, about as much excitement as being a Science Officer on a probe-cutter, where you have to have someone monitoring things constantly, but nothing happened very frequently. He'd frequently sat out at the edge of a system for a week or more, just plotting planets, comets, and asteroids before he ever got closer to the star. Suvi had handled all that, programmatically incapable of losing interest, getting bored, or taking a quick nap.

So it was like being home. Watching screens with about as much activity as mold growing or paint drying.

"So it really is easier not processing anywhere on the planet?" he asked Andak, mostly just to confirm everything Fritz had already told him.

"We're too efficient," Andak laughed. "Something like ninety-three percent of what's extracted gets used in the process. Smelted into bars, broken down to turn into dirt for stations.

Something. The rest gets brought back down and used as filler in permacrete to shore up walls and ceilings as we dig."

"Still think you should turn old mines into something useful," Afia muttered, just quiet enough that Andak could ignore her if he chose.

"We don't have the population pressures, Afia," he said back anyway. "Plus, people like living in domes with fish overhead, so we'd probably have to either bring in outsiders or put a huge effort into it. Still easier to add new domes undersea and stations in orbit. Besides, what would we do here?"

"You got a couple of botanists handy," she leaned forward now to look around Javier. "Galaxy's weirdest greenhouse?"

"We've considered it," Andak nodded. "But again, cost/benefit analysis has never penciled out. Stations have a purpose, either facilitating trade or providing industrial outposts with the added benefit of zero gravity. They tend to self-support. Short of putting in a company town down here, no way to really build an economy. Same with transportation. I'm sure a subway system would be more efficient, but people like their submarines too much, and all the cargo we might haul around goes up into orbit instead."

Afia grumbled a little but subsided. This wasn't the first time the conversation had chewed on that old bone, and the locals weren't inclined to do crazy things, just because some expert from out of town had a bright idea.

"So how much of your trade do you haul yourself?" Javier asked.

The concept of a company town triggered something in his lizardbrain, but it didn't want to come to the surface just yet. He poked at it some more.

"It requires a specialized vessel to connect to a mine and load ore," Andak practically beamed now. "We haul it all to orbit, and sell just under two-thirds to other conglomerates, rating load value with a formula that associates mass with volume being hauled. There are other mines owned by different folks that do much the same things we do here, so it all kind of works round-robin at the end of the day."

"Two-thirds?" Javier asked.

"Fritz has about four competitors up there significant enough to mention, besides me," Andak laughed. "We all specialize in producing different things, but there's enough overlap that the competition keeps people on their toes."

"What about after that?" Javier pressed, still niggling at something he couldn't quite get hold of. "Exports and such?"

He hadn't planned to meander down this particular alley. Certainly not with a cop two bodies to his left, straining to look casual now as she listened in and hoped for a smoking gun. Javier wouldn't have necessarily brought her, but he'd talked to Afia and understood his engineer's reasons, hokey as they might be.

"I don't have much in the transportation sector going out-system," Andak shrugged. "We have in the past, but it never really generated the sorts of profits we could get here, so I sold off most of those divisions about ten years ago."

"To whom?" Javier turned to the man. "Kept expecting you to try to hire *Excalibur* to haul cargo around."

Andak laughed. It sounded honest, too.

"People, maybe," he said. "I have considered a touring vacation, depending on what your next stops were. Bring along a jump-shuttle so I could get home later when I needed to, but like I said, most of my conglomerate stops at the edge of the solar system. There are a few moons we've considered burrowing, Afia, if you wanted to get involved at that end, but none of them have assayed out as good as what we could get here on *Ugen*."

"My apologies, then, Andak," Javier replied, "I seem to have picked up a misconception along the way. Fritz seemed to see you as a more direct competitor than you seem to see him."

"Fritz's great-grandparents had some mines on the sub-surface, but sold them off to Luo Industrial Products when they decided to concentrate on orbital stuff," Andak shrugged. "They actually built the first big smelters up there and got heavy into the export business. As far as I remember, he's still the biggest player in transportation that way, under about two dozen various corporations and seventy or so big hulls. We're happier down here making sure we make money from the ancient deposits, while keeping the oceans clean and healthy."

Javier didn't have to look that way to know that both Afia and Lan would have bad faces right now, if Andak looked. Well, maybe not Afia. Girl was a card sharp, but Lan would give something away if Andak looked, and the man was too smart to not see something.

And remember it later.

"So what about life support here on this mole vessel?" Javier asked, literally grabbing Andak by one arm and turning him the other way.

He aimed the two of them at Rainier and Emma now, like an extension of the previous conversation. Bethany had a confused face, but looked at him and went parade rest casual immediately.

Only Djamila had gotten serious. Hopefully she'd been paying attention enough to understand that Andak Luo wasn't any sort of threat to the group.

The man was being set up in one of the most professional and sophisticated scams Javier was sure he'd ever seen. And using a cop from the *Union of Man* to do it.

White hands, as it were. Plausible deniability later.

Pre-meditated self-defense, as the wag had once described it.

Javier didn't appreciate someone using him, though, especially not like this.

There was going to be a conversation with a few people, once he could get some privacy.

WATCHER

PART ONE

JAVIER GRABBED Afia as they departed the mine, the tour a successful afternoon of business, any other day. Didn't say anything. Just put a hand on her elbow and fixed his eyes on the tiny woman.

She'd played enough poker with him to nod silently and keep walking, still holding hands with Lan Cornish as she went.

Djamila nodded as well, but it was a different kind of nod. The pathfinders had picked up on the strange energy, as had Emma and Bethany.

And Rainier was still gabbing with Andak about plants and the benefits of an organic lifestyle, so they were hopefully both distracted.

He headed to his cabin and hung out for a little while, until he felt the yacht back away from the airlock and the mine, turning in place and then heading on to the next destination, an undersea forest of megakelp that Andak had promised to show Rainier and him.

Supposedly sufficient for commercial harvesting, if they wanted. Or maybe you could consider it old-growth around here, as there were places closer to all the domes, and not enough population density to push out much farther. An entire ecosystem evolving on an alien world.

Javier checked the clock. About an hour until dinner. Time enough.

He rose and made his way forward, assuming she'd be on duty now. Hopefully, the woman had recovered her equilibrium enough to have a misdirected conversation.

Andak was the only other guest likely to appear in the forward lounge, and he'd just spent the whole day with them, so hopefully the man would retire to his cabin aft and do business stuff for a while. Maybe even decide to skip dinner and send his condolences.

Javier couldn't talk in front of the two stewards that would be serving them, but everyone was probably a little raw and rough at this moment.

He should have known that Djamila would be here already, glass of wine in one hand. Bethany was doing a pretty good job pretending to be reading in a corner, but Javier wasn't fooled. Her eyes kept popping up at him as he entered and made his way to Lan's coffee stand.

"Ambassador?" she said politely as he got close.

Probably appropriate. Afia was the one she was fooling around with. As long as those two kept things discreet, Andak wouldn't say anything. Might fire her after the sub got back to the main dome, but they'd burn that bridge when they got there.

The case might have already been blown so wide open at that point that she'd be better off heading home to someplace like *Londra*. Or maybe infiltrating *Arsinoe* directly.

She'd most likely be done on *Ugen*.

"Decaf peppermint latte," he said quietly.

She wasn't working today with her usual impossible speed. Maybe to give them time to talk, even without significant witnesses.

"Enjoy the tour today?" Javier asked blandly.

"Exceptionally informative," Lan glanced up at him. "Especially those bits there at the end."

"I thought so, too," Javier nodded. "Who knew that intersystem transportation could be such a complicated and interesting topic?"

"Not I," she said as she was slowly, carefully pouring things together. Javier appreciated the complicated fern leaf she drew in the foam. "Personally, it inspires me to do more research on the topic."

"Ah, research," Javier leaned back as Lan handed him the mug. He might have raised his voice just a shade. "I happen to know an expert on the topic. Bethany is a Research Librarian, after all. That's why I hired her. She might be able to help you, if you get stuck looking for obscure information."

He turned and stared at the woman. Bethany tried to appear surprised as she looked up. Good enough, since they were alone up here.

He smiled to reassure Bethany and his unbloomed rose smiled back. She was getting there. Probably never going to turn her into a pirate, or even a freebooter, but she was coming around, and had taught Suvi and the rest of the crew all sorts of useful things.

After all, information was the hardest thing in the universe to find. Lots of data out there, but without coherence it was just noise.

Another reason he appreciated the Bryce Connection.

Bethany nodded at him now, acknowledging the conspiracy of silence that had stretched out in strange ways.

He needed to get everyone aboard *Excalibur* before he'd feel safe again, but as long as they played it cool, everything would be fine.

Javier moved over to a seat close to the Dragoon. Nodded to her.

"Messy," Sykora observed.

"Card sharp," Javier replied. Sit quiet and observe, as it were.

Sykora nodded. Sipped.

"Threat analysis?" she asked a moment later.

"That's your job, lady," Javier chuckled at her. "I hire killers so I don't have to do things like that."

"Our host seems remarkably open about things one would expect a tighter hold, in light of recent possible accusations," Sykora replied.

"I've considered faking a medical emergency of some sort," Javier murmured. "Just to give us an excuse to get out of the line of fire gracefully. Bamanie's feeding someone a load of hog shit and I'd rather not be collateral damage. The news would be too big if we did that, however, just on the count of me feeling paranoid."

"Cornish is on your side, as much as such a person from the *Union* might be," Sykora said quietly. "I can't speak to the other two."

"Someone is flat out lying," Javier glanced over at her with serious eyes. "I suspect it would take Bethany about ten minutes with the right terminal to identify which one it is. All that's going to be public record somewhere. Buried and obscure, but that's why I hired the woman."

"And then what?" Sykora asked. "Not our system. Not our government. No reason for us to remain involved once we board *Excalibur*."

That sounded like Djamila Sykora. Not quite mercenary, but not one to stick her nose in other people's business without a damned good reason.

Did political, economic, and social shenanigans qualify?

Javier wasn't sure.

PART TWO

Fritz looked at his handheld as the device beeped out. Called up the message.

"Dropped your package into the mail today."

Nothing more.

Nothing incriminating later.

No names. Just a system number that might possibly be traced back to someone working in one of Andak's mines. Perhaps sent to this number by mistake in the hurry to type it out.

Who knew?

Nobody could accuse him of doing anything. Of being involved.

It would all be a terrible tragedy that struck. That let him eliminate all manner of witnesses and rivals.

And nobody could trace anything to Fritz Bamanie.

Just terrible.

PART THREE

FOURTEEN YEARS active duty with the *Concord* Navy.

Ten years since then as a working spacer, first with *Mielikki*, then *Storm Gauntlet*, and now *Hammerfield/Excalibur*.

The sound brought Javier up from a dead sleep to full wakefulness between heartbeats. He was off the bed, throwing the cover back against the wall and standing, even before the echoes faded.

Two thumps. Dull, hollow. Followed by a hard spasm that passed through the entire body of the submarine.

Those had been explosions.

In space, you reacted instantly, because the next sound was frequently a hull breach and the whistle of atmosphere leaking. Hatches would slam shut as vacuum alarms came on, isolating frames and levels to minimize risk of a catastrophic failure. People would immediately move to soft suits, keeping the helmet at their hip until they had to face open space.

Except this ship was underwater. Water would begin leaking in rather than air out.

The lights went bright, and then failed. Emergency lighting ignited a moment later, paler and more yellow.

Javier sniffed, but didn't smell anything out of the ordinary.

Then he realized that the circulation system had shut down. As had the engines.

Then the submarine started to list to starboard.

Starboard roll ten degrees. Bow plane down twenty.

Javier grabbed onto the edge of the bed to keep his footing.

The submarine had just suffered a catastrophic failure.

His memory placed the explosions almost exactly below him and a little aft. Javier couldn't identify the sense that knew that, but a quarter century in space made those things automatic.

Sykora could probably tell you the exact mass of the explosive, had she been awake.

Maybe asleep. She was like that.

Down and a little aft. Muffled by an intervening deck where crew slept when they weren't on duty. Engine room. Life support generators. Mini submarine bay.

Yeah, I'd use two as well. Front and rear corners of the life support room. Blow it to hell. Flood the compartments ahead and behind.

It had been on the starboard side. The list was getting worse.

Forward motion felt like it was slowing, but the sub had been cruising at nearly fifty kilometers per hour before that. Not exactly racing to the next destination, but making sure they arrived just before sunrise so that the passengers could enjoy the sights before and after breakfast.

Starboard roll thirty degrees now. Bow plane still only down twenty.

Was she going to turn turtle on him?

A crunch forward caught his keyed up ears, even before the motion traveled the length of the ship.

Seamount.

We've just slammed into the side of a mountain. Dear Gods who love us, please tell me the bow held. If that goes, we're an eggshell leaking yolk all over the bottom of the sea.

At this depth, they'd all be crushed to goo, as well.

Javier found himself flying forward, thrown in spite of holding on. The fall wasn't far, and he saw it coming, so he turned as well as he could and relaxed.

Impact.

PART FOUR

THAT WASN'T RIGHT.

Suvi studied the scan results again and compared them to a handful of baseline records.

Still wasn't right. Whales don't do that, even when they're doing that bubble net thing to herd tuna into a trap.

She brought up the entire sensor suite and spent a few hours of personaltime tweaking and tuning things while aiming it at the surface. Maybe four seconds of realtime to a human, had any been paying attention.

Hammerfield had been built as a First Rate Galleon, a complicated mix of warship and cargo hauler. Flagship of the once-proud *Neu Berne* fleet.

But Suvi had been born aboard a *Concord* Probe-Cutter. The scouts. The eyes of the fleet. And Javier had spent a lot of his own personaltime adjusting her sensors to be even better than they had been.

That had carried over to *Storm Gauntlet* when Zakhar and the gang stole everything. Then *Hammerfield*, except that Behnam Sherazi, the Khatum herself, had paid to upgrade them again after *Nidavellir*.

Suvi was pretty sure there wasn't a better ship flying right now, when it came to scanning obscure and distant things and identifying them before anyone over there even knew there was an *over there* to know about.

Sneaky, like she liked it.

Those images didn't look right.

Something had just kind of erupted from the bottom of the sea, bubbling the living shit out of the surface over an area bigger than a hectare. Oil slick or something was forming. She couldn't get a good spectrographic analysis of it from here, but should probably wake someone up before she just left her current orbit to go on a fishing expedition.

The locals might get a little pissy. They could be like that, and it wasn't like she wasn't already making them nervous, being bigger, meaner, and tougher than any of them.

Hmmmm.

Mary-Elizabeth was sound asleep, and waking her didn't raise to that level yet.

Who else is around?

Piet had bridge watch right now, headphones on as he was composing something.

Hey, that sounds pretty cool.

Who else?

Why is Del still awake?

Still, he might know. Del was kind of an expert on crashes, and that looks a lot like a crash site, at least according to some of the records she was accessing right now.

She pinged him, not surprised to find him watching a vid from the flight deck of his nameless assault shuttle, seat tilted back and ankles crossed up next to the screen.

Suvi even understood why he refused to give the ship a name.

Delridge Smith only had a few known superstitions at this point.

Nothing Del had flown in the last generation, according to him, had gotten a name. All his previous fighters and shuttles, the ones to whom he had given names before that, had ended up dead in pieces somewhere. Better to not tempt the Fates any more. They had apparently appreciated his effort, because he'd turned into a crazy, gray-haired coot who still lived in Hawaiian shirts and decorated his flight deck like a *Merankorr* brothel, all pink fur, when almost all of his contemporaries were dead or at least long since grounded.

She opened a channel on his screen and presented herself in the top right corner as she paused his vid.

"Need your help with something," Suvi said in a gruff, no-nonsense kind of voice that Del appreciated.

"Talk to me, kid," he said, not stirring.

He was like that, too. But Del was seventy years old and had been flying combat vessels successfully for fifty of them. And while she was fifty years older, she still presented as a wet-behind-the-ears Yeoman, twenty-two years human standard. Cute and Nordic.

Rather than say something snarky, she swapped his screen image with her scanners, showing the complicated composite she was continually refining across every wavelength she could resolve from here.

"What's this?" Suvi asked.

"Ship crashed," Del said automatically. "Recently, but not that recently, because you'd have more stuff floating. Did you get an ID?"

Considering the number of shuttles, fighters, and other things he had crashed and still walked away from, Suvi was willing to take his word on it.

"There was nothing above the surface prior to this," Suvi answered. "Confirmed with all my logs. There are only about ten or fifteen things in the air at any given time, which is weird on any planet, but these folks like their submarines."

"Then you probably got a mayday situation," Del said. "Looks like a sub just imploded from the debris field."

Suvi wished she had a body sometimes, just so she could actually feel her soul go cold, instead of using it as a figure of speech.

Del noticed the pause.

"Talk to me, kid," he ordered now, finally dropping his feet off the dash and looking closer at her like he could read that frozen soul. "Why were you scanning this particular stretch of ocean?"

Hemming and hawing in her head didn't take long. He never noticed, unless he was reading her mind. Ya never knew with Del.

"The submarine that Javier and team was on left the mine at seventeen hundred local," she said. "Estimated course and speed to the next destination was known, so I've been kind of watching the vicinity with some spare sensor bandwidth. Saw this, but wasn't sure what I was looking at. I've never crash landed myself, except the time I broke that one guy's skull with my little flyer, and that doesn't count."

"Picked up a distress signal?" Del asked, actually rising now and turning from a kindly old man into an avatar of Odin, except for the two-eyes part.

"Negative, sir," Suvi said automatically, shifting into *Concord* Navy mode.

"Wake Zakhar right now," Del ordered her on a voice of doom from the blackest pits of hell. "Bring the ship to alert and shift our orbit around to establish a minimum-time insertion window."

Del was suddenly jogging, which almost frightened her more than Del as the angry patriarch.

"Where are you going?" She had to shift her voice around to the intercom on the stairs down to the flight deck to keep up with him.

"To prep *The Lander.*"

PART FIVE

JAVIER DIDN'T THINK he'd blacked out. Mostly just rested there for a few moments catching his breath. Car wreck without safety harness kind of thing.

Fortunately, nothing had spilled. That many years in space trains you to keep everything tied down, locked up, or stored in a cargo net automatically.

The submarine was laying on its starboard side, more or less. Not cleanly, but maybe sixty degrees list. Emergency lights were on. Nothing else.

It was eerie to Javier, listening to the perfect silence, broken only by the sound of his breathing.

He rose on unsteady feet and climbed up the hillside to his hatch. It hadn't sprung from the jarring, so he listened. No sound of water rushing in to drown him. That was good.

He rapped on it anyway, letting anyone out there know he was coming.

Someone knocked back and Javier pulled it open.

Of course Sykora would be up and about first. Fully dressed, including boots. He'd slept in bottoms and a shirt. That was good enough for now, except that shoes were probably a good idea. Broken things underfoot would be bad, even if the hull was intact. He grabbed a pair from the wall where they'd been stowed.

"Status?" she asked, eyeballing him in the dim light of the corridor.

"Bruised and battered," Javier answered. "No cuts. No concussion."

He was an expert on concussions. She'd given him several in a previous life.

"Is everyone awake?" he continued.

"Seeing to that now," Sykora replied. "We seem to have atmosphere here but I haven't checked other decks."

"You round up people," Javier said/ordered/decided/something. "Send me Afia when you find her. I'll check down decks first."

She nodded and continued. As Ambassador, Javier had the rear-most cabin suite, directly across from the one Andak was in. Sykora was rapping on his hatch as Javier headed farther aft.

The canted deck and emergency lighting made it almost more of an adventure than losing gravity on a ship. He got to the rear hatch across the hallway and peered through a window slot at eye level. Every submarine had them, so you would know if a chamber beyond it was flooded and not safe to open.

Just to be sure, he checked the environment system next to the door. Just exactly the opposite of a vacuum alarm but it showed green.

Behind him, he heard Andak responding to Sykora as she opened his hatch. Didn't sound like an emergency, so she could handle it for now. Other doors were opening farther forward.

He pulled this one up to open it and then let it drop shut behind him and set the seal once he was through, just like they trained you. A lifesuit would be nice now, but at this depth he'd probably need dive armor to survive a breach, so he didn't bitch.

Back here was the industrial side of the ship. They'd had a quick tour three days ago when they boarded. Andak's office was along one side, with some storage across from it and access to the conning tower. No carpet on this floor. Walls were painted, but showed scuff marks from people and equipment moving around.

Because he was not quite standing sideways, it took Javier a moment to orient himself and find the hatch down that he needed. The red light beside it told him all he needed to know.

Second deck was flooded. At least the section directly beneath him, which was a good chunk of crew quarters.

Javier wondered if the bastard who had planted those bombs had indeed put them at the top two corners of the life support space, so that the explosion blew out deck two at the same time it got deck three. How many people were down there dead right now? How many maybe trapped in their quarters and feeling the air grow steadily more stale because the air circulation vents had sealed at the same as the frame hatches?

At least in space, there was always a chance, if you were willing to risk vacuum exposure to get to an airlock. They had to be one hundred and fifty meters deep right now. Maybe more, except that they'd hit what felt like a mountain instead of dropping all the way to the sea floor.

But all the dive equipment was down on three.

Javier said a brief prayer for their souls and turned the other direction.

The conning tower showed green when he checked the sensors, so Javier pushed it open.

"Hello?" he called up the ladder.

"Here," a tiny voice answered from the darkness.

"Coming up," Javier said, and pulled himself up the ladder.

At least it was on the outer hull facing, so it was like walking up a weird flight of stairs to get to the control deck.

It was a mess up here. For a moment, Javier panicked, and then he realized that the liquid he was seeing was coffee that had spilled, rather than a greedy ocean that had already poked a hole in the dyke.

The man resting against the far wall looked hurt. One hand was pulled across his stomach and blood was dripping from a cut on his forehead.

Javier moved closer. He didn't know the crew, and had only seen Lan and a few others on the passenger side. This guy had a name embroidered on his shirt.

"How are you doing, Magee?" Javier asked as the man didn't rise.

"Broke things, sir," the man answered quietly. "Leg. Arm. Maybe some ribs. Maybe skull."

Javier studied him. They would need a stretcher to get the man out of this space, so maybe he'd send Afia up with the medical kit. She and Hajna were the two best at that sort of thing.

He checked the man closer, but there was only the one drip of blood on his forehead. Internal injuries were going to be beyond anything they could do right now. Except maybe give the man enough painkillers that he didn't feel death creeping up on him.

Hopefully it wasn't that bad.

Still, Javier found a towel and put it in Magee's good hand. Then he started touching the man. Magee was a trooper, and didn't once bite him.

"Okay, leg's probably broken, but feels clean," Javier told him. "Arm is just bruised, or maybe hairlined. Ribs are the same, but there's nothing to do with that except tape you for now. Follow my fingers."

Concussion protocol. Javier knew it well. But Magee was doing okay. Just got his bell rung pretty hard.

"Javier?" Afia called from below.

Beside. Whatever direction you used when a sub was laying on its side on top of a mountain at the bottom of the ocean.

"Grab Hajna and the medkit, Afia," he yelled back. "One injured male here needs you."

"Coming up," she yelled.

"You'll be fine, Magee," Javier said.

It wasn't a lie. If they could get out of here alive, he'd be with them. Might be the only crewmember Javier could say that about right now, without checking forward, so maybe it was Magee's lucky day.

If you could call this luck.

The women arrived a few moments later and Javier stepped back as they went to work.

He was more interested in the electronic systems around here right now.

The organic systems—the people—were trapped.

And if something good didn't happen in the next few hours, doomed.

PART SIX

DJamila had everyone rounded up, feeling like something of a queen bitch sheep dog as she did it. But they all woofed into place. Afia went to find Javier, returning a few moments later to get Hajna.

Everyone else had moved forward to the observation lounge. Djamila counted noses again. Andak Luo and a young female named Isaboe, neither of whom had been dressed when Djamila opened the man's hatch. Neither injured. The girl looked young enough to be his daughter, but of consenting age, and that was all Sykora ever enforced on any ship where she served.

Consent.

Both pathfinders were accounted for. Both Drs. St. Kitts. Bethany. Afia and Lan.

With most of the systems off, they had emergency lighting to cut the dimness, but it would start getting cold soon. Everyone was dressed, but hadn't brought heavy weather gear. Why bother on a submarine?

She would send Sascha for blankets in a while.

"Do we know what happened?" Luo asked as everyone got settled.

"I was awakened by what sounded to be twin explosions below my cabin, sir," Djamila replied. "One a little forward and one aft. If I remember your architecture correctly, I would place them high on the wall at either end of the life support plant."

"Why?" the man asked, still waking up and coming to grips.

"Breach both frames and both decks at once," Djamila answered in a technical tone. "Eliminate life support, engineering, and the diving well on the lowest deck. Take out a significant portion of the crew quarters on the middle deck, and most likely trap the remaining crew with flooding before they can respond and escape, if they knew where to go in such an emergency."

Andak Luo's eyes got big as he stared at her in unmitigated shock. But he didn't know her, except as Javier's bodyguard.

"As to why someone would wish to assassinate you, Luo, I can offer only a few theories, but we'll need Javier's input before we have that discussion," she continued with a frosty smile.

The two civilians recoiled like mice when the snake suddenly woke up. The others already knew the cogent pieces. And what kind of a woman Dragoon Djamila Sykora was.

Javier rescued the situation by arriving about then. Looking around, the couples were generally cuddled up along the downside wall, both for emotional as well as physical warmth. She nodded as the man staggered close on the pitched deck.

"Fore and aft ladders show crush pressure on the other sides of the hatches," he said simply to her, loud enough for everyone to hear. "Without dive armor and an airlock, no way to explore below for survivors or reach the important spaces at the bottom of the ship."

He paused and looked around.

"Sascha, you go aft to the conning tower and help your partner remove one wounded pilot," he ordered. "Bring Magee up here for now but have Afia stay put and start looking at systems so we know what we can do."

"On it," the pathfinder sprang up and headed out immediately.

Djamila always found it amusing that when a situation got deadly serious, then Javier Aritza turned into a proper naval officer. It would be nice if he did it more often, but it would also be lovely if it didn't have to happen as much as it had over the last few years.

She'd have been dead many times over if she had ever carried through her original plan to kill the man and make it look like an accident. It was kinda weird these days to have a big brother she could fuss with, but still respect.

Even a goofball like Aritza.

Javier counted noses like a good officer and nodded.

He turned to her now with a look of utter fierceness that was like someone else inhabiting the flesh. Not Navarre, but not that far removed.

Deadly intent.

Made her warm just thinking about it.

"Two charges?" he asked her. She nodded. "Shaped plasma lances? Inside or outside?"

"Why does that matter?" Luo spoke up now, still confused, but a rich man used to having a valued opinion on most topics because nobody had ever broken him of that habit.

"A spy trying to kill you versus a crew member embracing nihilism," Javier turned that immense, glacial rage on the man now.

"It felt outside," Djamila answered. "The pulse was coming up from inside the space and resonating through the sealed cavities."

He nodded at her.

When you've used so many types of explosives, to penetrate as many places as she had, you developed a feel for them. She'd never tried to assassinate a submarine that way, but the physics were similar enough when getting into a lamed freighter after your ion pulsars have shut it down.

Djamila had a lot of experience there.

"Why?" Luo asked again, almost like a broken record.

Hopefully his mind had survived the shock. Not everyone's did.

Javier pulled up an overturned chair and balanced on it precariously. He looked over at her but she shook her head to his unanswered question.

They didn't need words these days, weird as that was.

"So I have to tell you some things now, Andak," Javier began. "It had been my intent to wait until I was out of the line of fire and could do the necessary research, but that's past and you need the truth now, up front."

"What's going on, Javier?" Luo asked, his voice gaining strength now.

Rage catching the embers and bringing open flame, perhaps, but not the towering bonfire she could smell coming off Javier.

"So we started our tour on the station with Fritz Bamanie," Javier explained. "Spent some time up there and saw and heard some things. I need you to sit still and shut up right now, because I didn't need to apologize for it until now, but I'm angry and it isn't at you. Understood?"

The man scowled hard. Amazingly, the young girl next to him leaned in and just pressed herself against him enough to bring Luo's eyes around. Something unspoken passed between them, but it was obvious that the girl was more to the man than just a fling. And she had a brain in there.

Djamila upgraded her several notches.

"Okay," Luo agreed bluntly.

"So you have enemies," Javier continued. "Nasty ones. I doubt you're surprised by this, but one of them is going well above and beyond themselves right now and I get actively offended at being collateral damage."

"Who this time?" Luo asked, relaxing some, even as he started to wind to a higher level.

"One thing at a time," Javier assured him. "The *Union of Man* has decided to investigate smuggling originating out of *Ugen*, and sent an undercover police detective to get the goods on the problem at this end. I presume some sort of hard takedown at *Londra* or someplace, once they were sure, confiscating hulls and revoking trade licenses. Nasty shit."

"Not my problem," Luo growled.

"Correct, but we didn't know that until today," Javier nodded, backing his own emotions down as Djamila watched.

That was a skill she'd never mastered, but it was helpful watching a master do it, in case she needed to mimic him later.

"I don't understand."

"So Fritzie confronted me in space," Javier growled back. "Introduced me to said cop and pretty much blackmailed me into helping that investigation, if I wanted to continue having a pleasant trip in this system."

Djamila suppressed the smile that wanted to appear. Javier was shading the truth pretty hard, but that just told her that he'd figured this to be an assassination attempt, and who was likely behind it. And why.

Djamila would even apologize to the man, once she destroyed his organization, if they were wrong about Bamanie being responsible. She doubted she would ever have to consider such a thing.

Even if the rest of them survived, that cop, currently sitting uncomfortably next to Bethany, would have normally been on deck two.

And dead right now.

"Go on," Luo said in a dark, ugly voice.

"Luo, we're on your side right now," Djamila snapped, catching the man before his rage took over.

Isaboe also leaned more against him.

"So until yesterday, we were all of the opinion, based on other evidence largely supplied by Fritz, that you were the worst smuggler in the system," Javier said in a yet-lighter tone. "A kingpin of crime as it were. Then I asked you a question today and you blew everything up accidentally."

"I did?" Luo asked, breaking away from anger now as confusion crept back in.

"You innocently offered that you had sold most of your intersystem transport fleet off to Fritz about a decade ago," Javier nodded.

"Well, yes," Luo continued.

Then his eyes got dark.

"Bastard."

"Agreed," Javier said. "If the cops were looking for smugglers to break, you're about the last person on the list, I'm guessing. As soon as we got back to the main dome, I was going to have Bethany digest your corporate reports to confirm that. Once she did, the equations change and the investigation falls apart. But it makes a marvelous way for Fritz to take you and the cop out, make it look like an accident, and probably kill the ambassador involved. I don't know if he'd be dumb enough to try to capture *Excalibur*, but at a minimum he could offer a deal on things to Zakhar. I doubt he understands how badly that would fall apart, but we're here and he's not."

"Who is the gendarme?" Luo asked.

"Lan, join me," Javier called without looking at her.

Djamila watched the normally quiet and flirty barista stand and make her way over, except that now she walked like a cop.

Hard, cold, and deadly.

"Sri Luo, my name is Lan Cornish, and I am a police detective from *Londra*, in the *Union of Man*," she said simply. "My badge and papers are back at the main dome, but I have many people who can back up my story. And it flows as Ambassador Aritza has explained."

The man hissed angrily, but remained seated. Djamila wondered how much of that was her standing over everyone as a threat if he decided to get violent, and how much was Isaboe exerting all manner of soft charms on the man to keep him calm.

She might want to hire the woman later, if they all escaped all this. Those sorts of skills were always rare.

"Why would someone want to assassinate you, Andak?" Javier asked. "Well, what if they wanted to eliminate a cop who was starting to dig into your organization enough that maybe she discovers a truth that should remain secret? And maybe take you out at the same time? I'm guessing I'm just collateral damage, as I said. A useful plague vector bringing all this together and infecting you without realizing it."

"And my innocence?" Luo growled.

"I'm taking it as a given right now," Javier said. "Lan?"

"Agreed."

"There you go, Andak," Javier said. "Cards on the table and I'm sorry we all ended up here. I will owe you a much larger apology if and when we get out, but I'm personally going to have a long and *spiky* conversation with my old friend Fritzie. If he's lucky, he'll survive long enough for someone like Detective Cornish to arrest him. Or not."

Djamila watched Luo recoil a little under the force of Javier's rage.

Politics around here had looked soft, rather than the sorts of blood sport she had known in her time. Djamila assumed that assassinations were incredibly rare, from what she'd heard. That would make this one explode, if they could find a way out of here alive.

But this might just be an accident. One that might also set Fritz Bamanie up to pretty much take over everything for at least a generation.

Djamila was looking forward to strangling the man with her own hands.

"So now what?" Luo asked, settling his weight back some finally.

"Now I'm going to head aft and see if the systems we need survived and are operable for us to call for help," Javier said. "Emma, will you take charge of physiology? We need to preserve and extend our air as long as we can. Djamila, you look for any emergency oxygen generators we can trigger. We've got a long night ahead of us, and I'm not sure how long it will take potential rescuers to even know something's wrong."

Djamila moved, keeping an eye on Luo but trusting that Isaboe would help there.

She really wanted to get back to orbit. Not just to survive, but to have a chat with Fritz Bamanie.

MADMAN

PART ONE

IT DIDN'T HAVE A NAME. Not even *Nameless*, or some other cute whatever to get around not naming it. Sure, others called it *The Lander*, but Del flat refused. Never.

Every single flyable object he had ever given a name to had ended up scattered across somebody's landscape at some point. Him managing to walk away from the wreckage, or trigger the escape pod, or just blast clear in a flight suit didn't change the fact that *Fortuna*, Goddess of Luck, was offended by the act of naming a flying vessel under Delridge Smith's command.

Ergo, no name.

His usual home was a *Balustrade* Assault Shuttle, modified some but close enough to factory for government work. It had no name. Period. Fuck you for even suggesting it needed one.

The other vessel on this flight deck was really Javier's toy. He called it *The Lander*. Del refused. If pressed, he would use the damned thing's ID tag, painted in bright maroon on the gray hull in two-meter-tall numbers and letters.

But damn it, this thing was not getting a name. ***You can't make me.***

After long enough, even Javier had come around.

Del was about halfway through the pre-flight sequence on the secondary bridge when the inner airlock hatch opened. The thing still had the original flight deck, up a modified flight of stairs on the top level, but Javier had wired the damned thing so that it could be flown from the submarine swimmer that took up most of the original cargo bay.

Going to *Ugen*? Bring your own damned sub, except that the locals had flat vetoed letting an unknown vessel land in their oceans without a significant quarantine and inspection.

Del hadn't had a reason to push back that hard, since this system was sophisticated enough that Javier and folks could fly over to a station and catch a ride down.

He wasn't going to be asking today.

Zakhar was here. Interestingly, dressed for the field instead of in his usual pretty uniform that was *Concord* Officer with the badges removed.

The serial numbers filed off, as it were.

Del studied the man, the situation, the issue.

He toggled the comm on and found Suvi waiting for him.

"I need Ilan here immediately, with med kit," Del ordered, even before he talked to Zakhar. "And Dominguez as well."

"Yes, sir," Suvi said.

She didn't go anywhere, but Del understood that there were more of her than just the woman on screen talking to him.

"Were you going to ask?" Zakhar asked, taking the co-pilot chair and adding his hands to the preflight sequence.

"No," Del said.

Hey, might as well be honest here.

Zakhar turned to the Suvi image on a screen between them.

"Tell Piet he has command until I get back," the Captain said simply. "And not to take any shit from anybody. Understood?"

"Copy that," Piet appeared on the screen. "Do we alert the locals?"

"Not until I'm in the air," Del called. "Then tell them we are responding to a possible emergency rescue. I can get there faster than anything coming under water, and I'll also be dropping hotter than anything other than an escape pod coming off the station."

"Understood," Piet said. "Safe flight."

And he was gone.

Del worked hard and fast, but wasn't about to cut any corners. Not with as crazy as he envisioned the flight he was about to execute. Zakhar made it go faster, but nothing was going to make it fast, because nobody had expected to fly this thing after the locals objected.

Tough.

The inner airlock cycled. Ilan Yu and Mikhail Dominguez entered.

Del remembered the utterly hapless kid that had been assigned to Javier as a minder when they first conscripted the Science Officer to the crew. Any resemblance to Ilan of today was accidental. The man had flat saved Afia's life at *Nidavellir*, no two ways about it.

Del was hard pressed to think of anybody left on the current crew better than Ilan in an emergency, with Javier and folks downside.

"Dom, I want you in the topside bridge as a backup," Del ordered. "I'll be flying us down, so don't touch anything, but you'll have the shell once I deploy. From there, you'll stay close enough to be a relay and observation platform, and secondary rescue boat. If the locals get their shit together, you coordinate them instead of letting them be in charge. Questions?"

"Nope," Dom answered.

The kid was short and a little pudgy. More than Del. Kept his long hair in a brown ponytail most of the time, like now.

Wanted to be a chess grandmaster. Played the computer at a very high level, but Del didn't ever see him getting there. Dom was an intellectual player, not an artist. You needed that special something.

Same with flying. Perfectly capable pilot, but lacked that edge of luck and craziness that had let Del turn into an old man.

Del nodded anyway and Dom cycled himself out.

Ilan immediately headed aft and started checking supplies and gear. The Khatum, bless her soul, had given Javier a budget for his submarine, and that included dive armor and a special chamber if you had to rescue someone and bring them to surface pressure slowly, so as not to kill them from the Bends.

Del had figured at the time that they were being extra paranoid, but he was about to violate local airspace in a hotrod on a rescue mission, so what did he know?

"Bay has been depressurized," Suvi announced in her role as Flight Deck Master. "Rear doors are opening now and you are cleared for local space."

"Roger that," Del called back, taking a moment to check his harness before he started the ignition sequence on the generators and the engines.

"All hands, grab your ass," he yelled, trusting that these folks had flown with him enough times to know better than expect the sort of sedate ride a *Concord* Admiral might demand.

Del checked all screens before laying hands on the controls themselves.

Measure twice, cut once. Worked in wood just as well as flying.

Clear deck. Clear skies. Clear ocean.

Del brought the ship up onto her toes, broke deck contact, and spun in place.

Suvi had plotted his expected flight path, based on experience, and had the ass end of *Excalibur* already down and aimed at the piece of ocean Del wanted to visit.

He lit the engines and brought power slowly up. Zakhar still would have pitched a fit about flying too fast in the bay, except he was sitting in the next seat, watching controls but not touching anything.

Del cleared the aft lock hatch and slammed the throttle to the stops.

PART TWO

JAVIER LOOKED around the conning tower bridge, now that Afia and Hajna had gotten Magee out of the space and forward, where he could at least stretch out and get some serious pain meds in him.

Sixty degree right roll meant that he was standing on the side wall while looking at things, but the space was just about perfect. Afia was thirty centimeters too short to really work in here, so she was aft, where the sensors control was. Radar when the ship was on the surface. Sonar down here.

Dead as a nail right now.

"So where are the emergency batteries?" Javier asked, after clicking enough things to satisfy himself that nothing would turn on.

"Deck three with us," Afia replied. "That one storage closet that's only half deep has a wall of deep cycle batteries behind the shelves. Should be fully charged."

"So what's broken?" he asked, turning his head fully.

"Shit, I don't know, Javier," she snapped. "Could be any number of things. Hull flex pulled a wire. Same idiot sabotaged the power systems. Something."

"Assume bad luck," Javier said. "If he'd had a third bomb, we'd all be dead right now. Find a repair kit and start tracing things."

"What are you doing?" she asked, moving now to open drawers.

"Seeing if the emergency beacon is working," he replied. "I'd expect to hear it, unless it is too low for humans. But we'd feel it anyway."

She handed him a screwdriver multitool and Javier went to work. Spilled coffee might have just shorted something. Wires might have gotten pulled loose by the jarring impact of hitting a mountain. Whatever.

He got an access panel off and poked the tool in, using the little spotter flashlight on the tip to see. Everything looked okay, but who knew.

Instead of doing anything crazy off the bat, Javier started at the bottom left, pulling out every single wire, plug, or chip, wiping it off with his clean fingers, and making sure it was back all the way in. Maybe it had gotten dirty. Or knocked loose. Or something.

After the fifth board got reset, lights suddenly started blinking on the board. Javier pulled head back and looked at the dash. Sure enough, a little blinky red light wanted attention.

He shifted around to look at it.

Emergency beacon activate?

Oh, hell yes.

Javier mashed a finger onto the control, feeling it give just enough to bring him joy.

The whole hull seemed to ring like a bell for a moment as a triple chime sounded.

He'd never realized that submarines used the same sound as starships, but it made sense. Probably designed for starships and just installed here, as they were far more common.

"Hey, that's happy making," Afia called. "What was it?"

"Something loose," Javier said. "Hopefully someone's listening out there and can back track it to us with the equipment they'll need for a rescue."

"That thing reach space?" Afia asked. "Suvi hear?"

"No." He just shook his head. "Works best running along underwater, where the salinity of the ocean carries it, or something like that. Won't reach the surface with any power at all."

"Still something," she said with a smile in her voice.

"Something," Javier agreed. "How's power coming?"

"Tracing leads still," she said.

She did something and all of a sudden there was light. Sound, too, so apparently Magee had been playing music to keep himself focused.

Javier wasn't going to bitch too much about pastel jazz, but shut it down anyway. Every bit of battery power he could save right now.

"There we go!" she called.

"Good, now shut most of it down," Javier said. "Probably just strap yourself into the chair for now, unless you want me to do it."

"No, you can run errands up to the Dragoon," Afia laughed,

She did some gymnastics and was in the rear station, turned sideways more or less on her back as her fingers raced over the keyboard.

Most of the lights went back off.

"Observation deck, this is the bridge," she said into a comm line. "Battery power on, but we're going to keep most things powered down for now, including heat. Make sure to grab all the blankets and warm clothing."

Javier nodded. He turned to the navigation system and got it on line. Green lines tracing depth showed the shape of the ocean they had been traversing. Mostly flat, but right at the edge of a ridge. He called up the map and whistled.

"What?" Afia asked.

"Have a look," he said, mirroring his readout to her screen. "Five more minutes and we'd have been on the other side of this mountain we hit."

"This is the continental shelf edge," Afia gasped. "Shit, how deep is it over there?"

"Four thousand meters in a few places. About a thousand, anywhere we would have landed."

"This thing survive that depth?"

"Not a chance, kid," Javier said grimly. "We'd have been a tin can run over by a lifter down there."

"Small victories," Afia said quietly.

The hull pinged again with the triple chime. Okay, going off every minute. Good enough to notify people.

Javier assumed whoever was supposed to race to the scene to rescue them would have found the ship down in the impossible depths. The kind of place where you'd need extremely specialized dive armor to get to, or a super-tough submarine for rescues.

More than any casual submarine who happened to be in the area would have had when they came to save you.

Somebody had wanted Andak Luo dead. And Lan Cornish. And oh, by the way, Javier Aritza was going to be unfortunate collateral damage.

Somebody was going to get theirs when he got out of this, *Nidavellir*-style.

"So now what?" Afia asked.

"We got secondary life support systems?" Javier asked. "Or alternative heating that doesn't burn battery?"

"Negative on both," Afia replied grimly after a few moments. "Everything was apparently down on the lowest deck and is showing red on my boards. Emergency equipment is forward in the observation lounge in a closet and that's about it for now.

"Okay, you stay here and monitor for incoming signals indicating rescue or anything." Javier started to move. "I'll send someone to keep you company, but minimize power use as much as you can. Let me know if you hear anything."

"Will do."

Javier climbed down the staircase to the passenger deck.

They were dead on the sea floor, in the middle of nowhere, using power and at risk of freezing to death or suffocating. At least they were shallow right now, and alive.

Somebody could do something.

All he had to do was survive long enough to exact his revenge.

PART THREE

BETHANY HAD OPENED the closet with all the emergency stuff and started cataloging it against the checklist on the inside of the door. Oxygen candles. Self-contained heater unit, single use, six of. Food tins and a can opener.

Wonder of wonders, none of it was even close to expiring, unlike a few of the ships she had sailed on in her midshipman days.

She took a can in hand and walked over to Luo, holding it out as she got close.

"Thank you," she said as the man looked up at her in surprise.

He was as old as her dad, but hadn't looked it until now. Under the tan and vibrancy, he was gray and haggard right now.

Bethany wondered how much of his appearance was cosmetic.

"For?" he asked in confusion.

Bethany handed him a can of crushed pineapple.

"For not cutting corners and being a cheap shit," she said. "Check the date."

"Expires in seventeen months," he said without conviction.

"On a lot of *Concord* ships, you'd be lucky if it had *only* expired seventeen months ago, sir," Bethany nodded. "So I wanted to let you know that I appreciated you not cutting corners on things. All the supplies are up to date, so presumably they work and we gain time."

"Oh," he said, brightening. "Thank you and you're welcome?"

Bethany nodded with a smile and turned to Djamila now.

"How soon should we light an oxygen candle?" she asked. "We have six."

"Let the air get a little more stale for now," the woman decided.

The entire ship chimed. Everyone jumped.

"What was that?" the woman Isaboe asked, obviously frightened by the way she clung to Luo's side.

"Emergency beacon activating," Bethany smiled at her. "Should have gone off immediately, but something wasn't right."

A moment later, lights came up in the room.

"Observation deck, this is the bridge," Afia's voice came. "Battery power is on, but we're going to keep most things powered down for now, including heat. Make sure to grab all the blankets and warm clothing."

There was a small cheer from everyone.

Djamila signaled to Hajna and Sascha and those two jogged out, presumably to strip beds and stuff. Magee was on a pile of pillows from the sofa right now, stoned to his gills and sleeping.

Before Bethany could decide where to move off to, Lan Cornish walked close. The woman nodded up to Bethany and faced Luo.

"Unlike Bethany, I owe you an apology," Cornish said to the man. "Several, in fact, but before I do that, I also wanted to tell you that you've been one of the best bosses I've worked for."

"Really?" Luo asked.

"Oh, I'm sure you'd have hauled me into your office and fired me, once we got back to the main dome," Lan chuckled. "Unacceptable fraternization with passengers or something and that's fine, but you've been cool about everything, and I wanted to say thank you."

"You are welcome, Lan Cornish," Luo said slowly and

distinctly. "At least we'll all have clear consciences when we go to hell for other reasons."

"I'm not planning to end here, Luo," Lan said as Bethany watched the woman transform from polite barista to hard-ass cop in just a few syllables. "Javier and the others aren't either. When we get back to the dome, my investigation continues, but now I'd like to apologize for not digging deeper into your public records earlier. Bamanie apparently has everything hidden behind shells and I didn't dig deep enough to catch where you had quietly sold everything off. Instead, I listened to his pretty lies. He was using me to destroy you, and lying to me every step of the way."

"And assassinating me? You? Us? Everyone?"

"I expect that he knew I would find the truth out here," Lan said. "Enough truth, anyway, to put him at risk. Someone at the mine had it in for us, so he has spies and assassins on his payroll. We survive this and he's going to have all sorts of investigations crawling up his asshole with a microscope, and that's just me. How do you suppose the system government will react to the news that someone tried to assassinate an Ambassador from *Altai*? In addition to Andak Luo?"

"That will get ugly," Luo noted in a dry voice. "Doubly so when it comes out that Lan Cornish is a *Union* gendarme. I have a small enough soul that I might be looking forward to watching all of that unfold. Assuming we do get home."

Bethany decided that she liked the guy, after all. She hadn't been sure, earlier. A little too pompous and full of himself had been her initial impression, but after a few days he had relaxed some.

Of course, anybody having to spend time around Javier would start off nervous. He was like that. She remembered.

"So for everything, I apologize," Lan said with a half bow that really conveyed sincerity. "I cannot make up for the other things, but I promise you my investigation will change direction completely and focus on players above the atmosphere."

"Thank you," Luo said quietly. "It is nice of all of you to

assume that we will make it home alive that such plans could be made with an expectation of execution."

"Andak, has anyone ever told you you're too sour?" Javier called as he stepped into the lounge.

Bethany's head came around just like everyone else. The man knew how to make an entrance.

"We've got power," Javier smiled at everyone. He glanced at the open closet where Bethany had been working. "We got air and heat for a while. I'm sorry if we can't save anybody from the lower decks, but I fully plan to get out of this alive and go blow up somebody's life for this."

"You seem sure of yourself," Luo said.

"Worse comes to worst, I'm pretty sure I can hotwire your comm system to send a message," Javier said.

"The current system will only reach the main dome," the man replied, confused.

"Yes, it will," Javier nodded.

Bethany was also confused by the noncomment, but she recognized the look in Javier's eyes right now.

She hadn't been with them at *Nidavellir*, but she'd heard the stories around the dinner table, and as Ship's Historian she had interviewed Suvi and Captain Sokolov. Javier wasn't talking about letting the locals know there had been a problem.

He was wishing he could brief Suvi and Sokolov directly. And then let them loose on Fritz Bamanie with a warship capable of destroying everything that man owned, consequences be damned.

Worse?

She was looking forward to it.

PART FOUR

ZAKHAR KEPT his eyes on the pressure gauge and various temperature sensors around the hot parts of the hull. He was just glad that Del knew the limits of the ship as they had bombed down into the atmosphere red hot.

Probably, the madman had just shaved five or ten years off the functional lifespan of this second assault shuttle, but that was an acceptable trade, if they got Djamila and Javier and the rest home.

"Grab your ass," Del said conversationally.

Zakhar pulled his hands off the keyboard and leaned back into the seat, buckled in tight, but you never knew what Del was going to do when he gave you that kind of warning.

The shuttle had been sixty degrees down angle, punching a hole through the atmosphere like a bullet. Del had only backed off when Zakhar started calling temperature ratings out loud.

And not even that far.

Just enough that they didn't melt anything critical.

Now, the shuttle turned on one side and the glide wings finally deployed. It was like a parachute opening as the ship snapped down hard and then entered a spiral, standing on one wing.

Zakhar took a couple of moments and let his stomach settle before he tried speaking again.

"Six thousand meters and descending," he called, just in case Del didn't know that measurement instinctively.

Nobody had ever figured out how Delridge Smith worked. It was enough that he was the craziest, best pilot Zakhar had ever met in a career of being a professional spacer.

"Dom, start your checklist," Del spoke again, talking to the backup pilot upstairs in the outer shell.

The one that they would leave behind when *The Lander* submarine element detached.

"Ilan, you ready?" Del said a little louder, speaking to the man behind them.

"Cloth tape and hammer," Ilan called back with a chuckle.

It was only slightly humorous. At *Nidavellir*, Ilan's quick thinking with an entire roll of engineering tape had been the difference between Afia surviving and being buried in space, when one of the other pirates had opened fire on an escape pod and hit it just hard enough to drive a chunk of steel into the woman's stomach.

Zakhar smiled to himself at the memory. Nobody had ever given the kid credit for potential. They had only seen the raw, untrained rookie, not the brains and self-confidence that had just needed the right mentor.

Who would have imagined that it would have been Javier Aritza?

"Five thousand meters and descending," Zakhar called out.

"Suvi, confirm coordinates," Del said aloud.

Zakhar was just the co-pilot today. This was Del's ship. His mission.

Him and Suvi.

Maybe the craziest combination of flyers you were ever going to find.

A red cross appeared on the screen between them, showing the map overlay where his favorite yeoman had been a moment ago.

"Circle of possible error is four kilometers across," she said. "I have tried to account for tidal currents, depth, and salinity, but there is a small range of undersea mountains running across your search zone, right before it drops off the continental shelf."

"Bring me in from the shallow side," Del called. "Easier to look with eyeballs when we get to depth."

"Roger that."

Zakhar watched the screen shift again, a series of vectors showing now, adjusting constantly as the shuttle flew.

"Four thousand meters and descending."

Del flattened them out now, pointed into what would be the rising sun if they flew far enough.

If you were in an atmospheric landing, this would be what they called the *Downwind* leg, where a flying vessel went past the runway once to confirm everything and to be seen on the ground.

"Three thousand meters and descending."

Del must have decided he was far enough out, because his hands suddenly began dancing across the controls.

"Stand by for subsonic flight," Del announced, pushing the throttle forward and letting the shuttle nose up just a little as he deployed flaps.

"Two thousand meters. Descent slowing."

Wonder of wonders, Del went into *Baseline* almost sedately for once, turning onto one wing and bleeding off velocity as he came around and lined them up for a spot on the surface.

The air outside was cold, but clear. About the best they were going to get at this latitude and season. Not that a full-on blizzard would have mattered, other than Del would have done all this on instrument rules only, and not been able to impress whatever sea-dwelling birds happened to look up right now.

"One thousand meters and descending," Zakhar called, studying his screens for all the secondary tasks that Del might be too busy to consider right now.

The shuttle came to a stall and started down like a rollercoaster at the top of that first, crazy arc. Again, Del in a hurry to get troopers on the deck while under hostile fire.

At least nobody was firing at them. Zakhar didn't think much would change in that sort of scenario, except that Del might have brought Mary-Elizabeth down and put her forward in the pulsar turret to clear a landing zone.

They'd have still made a combat drop.

"Five hundred meters," Zakhar called.

"Dom, what is your flight status?" Del called professionally.

"All systems green, Del," Dom called back a moment later. "Standing by for secondary flight."

"Two hundred meters," Zakhar said. "Descent slowing."

They were falling almost like a feather now, compared to the mad race to the bottom of the well that had marked the last two hours.

The whole vessel shuddered now as Del rolled up the glide wings and relied entirely on thrusters vectored down. Inefficient flight, but the best way to hold a perfect spot on a featureless ocean.

Zakhar shifted the scanner now to showing the horizon relatively flat.

"Wave swell under three meters," he called, just in case Del couldn't smell what the ocean goddesses were up to today. "Visibility forty kilometers."

The shuttle came to a dead hover at about ten meters, held there for a long moment.

"Dom, deploy flotation gear," Del called.

They could do it from down here, but better that Dominguez was controlling things now. If all went well, he would be in command shortly.

Around the bottom of the outer hull, skirts and inflatable bladders deployed, hissing as they filled with air.

"Landing apparatus shows green," Dom called a moment later.

"Zakhar, start your unlock process," Del said.

Again, Del could have done it himself, but he had three spare sets of hands to do things right now, and Delridge Smith was in command. He didn't cut corners flying.

Zakhar started the process. Javier had designed it with help from various teams. Even tested it several times.

"All systems show green," Zakhar said after a moment.

"Dom, lower the winch," Del commanded.

The shuttle was only held in place now by a series of four thick hawser cables, emerging from the corners of the bay to a magnetic grapple that locked into the center of gravity of the submarine. Zakhar had unlocked all the places holding them up once Mikhail Dominguez had opened the plates shielding the vessel itself from reentry heat.

They began descending. The wind wasn't bad, so they didn't rock all that much as they lowered. Mostly surface effect from waves constantly moving, but not enough to cause anyone an upset stomach.

Not if they'd already survived this long.

The submarine touched water with a soft splash.

"Dom, hold here."

Del brought thrusters live and vectored everything for a moment.

"All controls show green," Del announced. "Dom, detach the grapple and return to your patrol."

"Detaching grapple now," Dom called.

The shuttle fell at least a meter as they were suddenly on their own. Not enough that the camera Zakhar was using was submerged, but the splash was big.

A whale deciding to erupt from the depths and cannonball someone on the surface.

"Submarine One, what is your status?" Dom called the cadence.

"Submarine One in free flight and responding to all controls," Del answered.

"Godspeed, Submarine One," Dom called and then backed away from them on thrusters, the spider web retracting into his belly as he went.

Del looked over with a cold smile.

"Time for you to get into the dive armor, Zakhar," he said ominously.

PART FIVE

Del dialed the crazy back a notch as they hit water.

Okay, half a notch. More or less.

Zakhar and Ilan were aft in the dive airlock getting geared up for some craziness. Suvi was going to be harder and harder to reach as he got deeper, unless he wanted to deploy that relay float on the tether.

Maybe later. It would slow him down too much right now. And speed was still the most important thing he could bring to the table.

So he lit the sonar and scared the hell out of anything even remotely close by, but that was fine. The more the fishies got out of his way, the easier it would be to scan the bottom and see what he was looking for.

A triple-ping emergency beacon nearly levitated him out of his seat, harness or no harness.

Del cranked the radio transmitter to stupid levels and held elevation for a moment.

"Suvi, have just received a distress signal," Del said simply. "Vectoring down on it with my own beacons live."

Her image on the screen next to him had that washed out feel you got when she left an image there instead of actively inhabiting it.

"Understood," came the response, at least that was what it sounded like through the hash.

Del cranked the scanner now and sent a pulse downrange to let whoever know that help was coming.

"Hey, guys, I have a distress call," he said into the radio channel Ilan and Zakhar were on.

"Heard that here," Ilan replied. "Keep us posted."

The undersea was a long, flowing set of hills. If he'd been in a gunfighter right now, just the perfect sort of terrain to drop to *Nape of the Earth* and blast in on somebody too low for ground-based sensors to track him. Unless they had a tower scanner sitting high enough for radiation missiles to put paid to it.

Del missed the crazy days when people paid him to strafe pirate bases on hidden colonies. Javier kept talking about a war coming, but Del just knew he'd be dead before the good stuff happened and he got to return to the glory days of a half century ago.

Probably just as well that this submarine wasn't armed with any torpedoes or such. Del figured he'd get a little out of hand occasionally, just from temptation. Although maybe somebody would hire Zakhar out for that and he could load the ass end of this submarine up with assault swimmers in little jet pods.

Another ping cut through the seas.

Del turned his nose into the current and pushed the bow planes down.

Time to go hunting.

PART SIX

Lan studied the group around her as they waited. Despair had not set in, in spite of what she had expected. Maybe Javier was just too much alive to die that easily.

Djamila had ordered Bethany to light one of the oxygen candles at the same time she had covered over the open hatch with a blanket. That way they didn't have to use power to cycle the door, and it kept heat in.

The first of the heater elements was silently emoting in the middle of the room with a blinking light to let everyone know that it was on. As if the warm breeze circulating wasn't enough of a clue.

Andak Luo got up from Isaboe's arms and walked closer, a hesitant look on his face.

Lan looked around and all the others were occupied with their own thoughts, although both Djamila and Bethany had tracked the man.

"May I?" he asked, gesturing to the chair where Lan kept hoping that Afia would come keep her warm.

Javier had sent Sascha instead of her aft to where Afia was working. Probably didn't trust her, in spite of everything.

Or because of it.

"Please," Lan nodded to the man.

He sat and studied her. She had put on two more shirts and a pair of sleeping trunks over her pants, so she was warm even though the room was only in the high teens right now. Luo had a jacket on and that seemed enough.

"So you're a spy?" he asked.

Wasn't hostile. Curious, maybe. Something.

"A cop," she corrected him. "Deep cover detective on a long-term mission to identify the parties behind a serious smuggling problem affecting the economy of *Londra* and other *Union* worlds."

"Same thing," he shrugged.

Lan couldn't really argue with that. The craft was similar. It was just the target that varied.

And the rules.

A spy could be caught, but they were diplomatic agents, so usually they would get arrested, blown, and deported. Or maybe traded for someone else, depending on conditions in the outer world.

A cop was much more likely to be chucked out an airlock or shot in the head in a dark alley.

"Why?" Lan asked when the man lapsed into silence.

"I'm a businessman," Luo replied after a moment.

Lan just stared at him, daring the man to speak.

"I presume that your cover is largely blown at this point," he finally spoke. "I know who you are. Fritz knows. If he's the one trying to kill you, you won't be able to go undercover into his organization after this, so there's not much left for you to do."

"True," Lan agreed, not willing to cede this man much.

"So I have a couple of propositions to run by you," Luo said, his face clearing up to something less dangerous-looking than what he had brought over.

Lan didn't scowl, but also didn't say anything. Rich, old men with young, bimbo girlfriends along for a sail didn't impress her when they started talking about propositions.

"One, it's obvious that the law enforcement authorities on this planet don't seem to be up to snuff, if the *Union of Man* had to infiltrate *Ugen* in order to get something done," Luo continued, watching her and waiting for a response.

Lan nodded. That had been one of the first things her bosses has stressed, two years ago when they brought her in to discuss this mission.

"So how would you feel about being recruited to some sort of extremely senior position on *Ugen*?" Luo asked. "*Directora*, if not Police Commissioner herself?"

"Really?" Lan asked, trying not to pour sour milk all over the word as it came out of her mouth. Probably unsuccessfully.

"Clean slate, Detective," Luo said. "I do not figure that I am going far out on a limb to suggest that the current Directors and Commission probably cannot not survive an investigation into their own behaviors. It just never seemed to matter to us on *Ugen*. Each generation seemed to bring a different set of hotheads to run the system, but it never changed anything in the depths."

"Would they even accept a *Union* cop?" Lan asked snidely.

"No, you'd have to become an *Ugen* citizen for something like that," he nodded knowingly. "Big step. Maybe more than you are interested in, because I doubt anybody has ever asked about whatever home life and family you might have left behind."

Lan was impressed with this man's recognition of that. She didn't have a family to speak of. That was why they had chosen her for this mission. The big promotion when she came home successful wouldn't be anything equivalent to even Detective Lieutenant, to say nothing of one of the political jobs Luo was mentioning, but still.

"And what was your number two?" she asked, just to see how Andak Luo might top that.

"It's a little more complicated," he grinned wryly. "If this breaks Fritz, then maybe Luo Industrial Products needs to reconsider getting out of the transportation business. Especially if *Ugen* Export Services suddenly has to have a fire sale. I would need folks I could rely on to work with *Union of Man* officials as

I started transporting goods again, especially to places like *Londra*. It would be a civilian job, rather than gendarme, but the pay would be commensurate with a division director here, which is probably ten times what you were making back home."

"Rely on?" she asked, a little incredulous.

Twelve hours ago, she had been a barista assigned to his secondary yacht. A cover, but a damned good one. With pretty good fringe benefits.

"You had to be amazingly competent to be picked for this in the first place, Cornish," he said. "And scary enough to Fritz that he turned himself inside out to aim you at me. Dangerous enough that now he has decided he has to kill you. Good enough to convince Javier and the others to cover for you, even if they were being blackmailed, because any of them could have made you disappear if they thought you were a threat to Javier."

Lan blinked in shock.

She'd never put it together like that.

Andak Luo just smiled at her.

"Uhm," she kind of stuttered back at him.

Luo nodded and rose.

"Take your time," he said. "Javier is convinced we're getting home, so I have to begin rearranging my plans for tomorrow. I decided to start with you."

He walked away before Lan could come up with anything pithy to say.

Talk about a heavy load. Lan had been pretty sure she was going to be lined up and fired, maybe blackballed five minutes after Javier and everyone departed.

Now he was offering her two different kinds of brass rings, if she was crazy enough to take a shot at either of them. Did she want to?

Lan held her breath and wondered what silly thing Afia might whisper in her ear were she here right now. That was an even weirder option, if she really wanted to catalog them all in one place.

Sykora was staring at her from across the room right now,

like maybe Lan was broadcasting thought bubbles for everyone to read.

She stopped herself before she actually looked up.

What did she want?

To get home, but Lan had no idea where home might be right now.

PART SEVEN

AFIA JUMPED when the hull pinged.

That was sonar blasting from close by, if she understood how sound waves worked underwater.

"Mayday mayday," she announced in a calm voice as she opened the radio and set it to broadcasting.

Sascha jumped even harder, but stayed quiet, face all sorts of surprised.

"Didn't I warn you about going to those kinds of parties, kid?" a kindly voice suddenly came back on line.

DEL?????

Holy shit!!!

"How'd you get here?" she asked.

Afia stopped hyperventilating long enough to open the ship-wide intercom so the folks up on the bow would hear.

Oh My GOD!!

Sascha leaned over and hugged her for no other reason than they were alive.

"Suvi saw something that didn't look right," Del answered her with a smile in his voice. "I hot launched and brought the other shuttle down to see what you needed. Anybody tell you that you aren't supposed to park a submarine on the side of a mountain?"

"You ain't heard nothing yet, Smith," Afia laughed. "How close are you?"

"Coming alongside in about ten minutes," Del said. "What is your status?"

Afia took a long, deep breath.

"Explosions took out decks two and three on the starboard side, mid and aft," Afia said in a quieter, harder voice. "Both appear to be flooded. We are running on battery power with emergency gear. Our team plus four others are forward in the observation dome. One serious injury. Everything else was minor. Ship is listing sixty-three degrees to starboard but generally flat linear."

"Roger that," Del said. "Coming up on you at about one hundred forty degrees right now. I have two divers I can put down, but it looks like you will be able to cross via airlock?"

"Conning tower has a lock we can use at the top," Afia replied. "Shirt sleeves environment, but the one will need a stretcher."

"Got one in my gear," Del said. "I'll have it in the airlock when we dock. ETA five."

He cut the line and Sascha screamed once with pent up energy.

Javier was standing there when Afia looked, smiling ear to ear, but she'd allow him that. The damned thing Del was flying had been his idea in the first place. His baby, even when everyone else didn't believe.

"Good job," Javier said.

Afia leapt up just to hug the man. For lots of reasons.

"So we're starting everyone aft," he continued. "Sykora is bringing Magee, so we may not need the stretcher until we cross, but I'll leave that to Sascha and Hajna to determine."

"We're going to do it," Sascha whispered fiercely.

"What have I told you about lacking faith?" Javier grinned at her.

"Oh, sure, inject male ego here," Sascha laughed at the man. "Whatever."

Afia laughed.

God, it felt good to be alive.

Bethany stuck her head into the bridge with a look that suddenly brought Afia back to earth.

"Javier, someone's alive on two," Bethany said. "I just heard them banging on the hull with something metal."

RESCUER

PART ONE

DEL SMILED as he realized that no craft he had ever flown could pull this stunt, hanging ass down twenty degrees while hovering thirty meters above the deck. Granted, submarine, but still.

Shit, he'd have to give Javier even more credit. They were perilously close to swelling that boy's head already.

"Ilan, what is your status?" Del called on the local radio channel to his divers.

On the screen, they looked like a pair of giant crabs swimming in the water. Sharks were all streamlined and stuff. This gear looked like a pack of armadillos fornicating, just to watch the arms and legs flail around. That armor was heavy. Mass required a lot of muscles, and these were only partially powered exoframes.

"Connecting the cables now," Ilan replied with a grunt.

Del watched the rear cameras with a smile.

Javier was insane, but that was nothing new. After airlocking everyone aboard from the top deck, he wanted the sub to pull the wreck vertical to see if they could rescue others.

So Ilan was introducing Zakhar Sokolov, of ALL people, to sub-EVA techniques.

And Javier had included a winch for this sort of thing, except Del had always figured that it was really for looting sunken treasure ships, like maybe Drake would have done, once upon a time, rather than Cousteau.

And a harpoon gun, but they couldn't use it today, as they had an actual pressurized environment below them. Bad time to punch holes in it.

Ilan had the cable played out, looped all the way around the conning tower below the upper maneuvering planes, and Del was supposed to drag the damned thing just enough to right it, without tumbling the bastard backwards down the hillside where it might just break up.

Del turned and looked at the party of lunatics he had rescued. Everyone from *Excalibur*, plus some.

He chuckled at the thought of Javier and Sykora both making it out alive.

There had been a time.

"Javier, a spare pair of hands up here would be nice," Del announced as everyone settled and the medics did their thing.

"Bethany's a better pilot than I am," Javier replied, waving the newest crew member over.

Del liked the way she blushed for all of two seconds, took a deep breath, nodded to the universe, and then sat where Zakhar had been keeping him company before.

"What do you know about undersea maritime recovery operations, kid?" Del asked.

"You have a two hour head start on me," she retorted with just enough sass to make him smile.

About right.

"Your job today is loadmaster," Del said, sobering significantly as he took the situation in. "You own the winch and the weight at the end. I'm just flying, but we use the thrusters to move things around. If we lose the cable, I need you to back the tension off the line fast enough that nothing snaps back and cracks my hull. Questions?"

He liked the way she called up several images now, ignoring him completely as she worked.

"What happens if you swing your bow around about three

to five degrees starboard before you put tension on it?" Bethany asked.

Damned good question. He looked.

"Yeah, that probably holds the other sub in place better by driving the bow deeper into the mud as she rolls," Del agreed. "I'll shift once the divers are clear and you're ready."

"Acknowledged," Bethany said, never once looking up from vector diagrams.

Okay, so maybe she was going to be better at this than Javier. That was good. It would keep that boy merely mortal.

Can't have a demigod as a Science Officer. Could you imagine the future legends that might accrue about the man's name if they let that shit happen?

"Del, this is Ilan," the call came back. "We're set here and backing off to the north to clear your path. Don't forget to come back for us."

"You still owe me money, kid," Del laughed at the man doing all the hard work.

The rest of them were mostly just along as witnesses. The strangers trapped on the sub would live or die on Ilan Yu's brains and skill.

As frightening as that would have been five years ago.

"All hands, buckle yourselves in tight," Del said loud enough to cut the chatter behind him.

The injured dude was tied down enough that he wasn't going anywhere, and out cold anyway. The rest needed to do more than just grab their asses right now.

He even turned to take everyone in and count noses before he looked at the vectors Bethany Durbin had called up and calculated. Yeah, she had a better understanding, but only at an intellectual level.

She'd never flown a strike fighter into the side of a mountain above water and then hiked three days to an extraction point with a broken arm. Not many people had.

Ilan and Zakhar were clear. He brought the thrusters up a single notch, just to tighten everything as he slewed the bow around to line up with what the Historian had in mind.

It was a shame that Del had never had kids. Bethany Durbin was the kind of woman he'd have wanted to introduce a grandson to.

Of course, he'd have then had to explain what Grandpops did for a living.

"Bringing cables tight," Del said to her as he kept everything focused on the screens.

The craft buckled a little now. Nobody had any idea what kind of muck and mud the other submarine was resting in, or how hard it would be to roll the thing just a little.

Should be enough mass to let him shift everything about ten meters and call it good. The fear was rolling it all the way over to the other side.

Or tumbling it backwards down the slope and killing whatever poor bastard had managed to survive this long, trapped in his cabin by the flood waters.

"Diverting power to the thrusters," Del said calmly.

Just another day at the office.

The hull began to vibrate. Good sign. Everything held cleanly and the cable was plucking a low G.

"Status?" Del asked.

"All vectors still aligned," Bethany said in a forced voice.

But then, she'd been a career librarian, not a madman. Made a world of difference.

"More power," Del said, tapping the controls exactly once and then pulling his hand clear.

"Del, I see movement," Ilan called.

Damned kid shouldn't be close enough to the wreck, but maybe there were enough lights to show motion?

Del grunted and poised his hand on the thruster controls again.

He was flying by feel, but that was nothing new. Sometimes you had to turn off the stupid targeting computer and trust your own instincts to launch torpedoes, especially when you were flying right down on the deck where pedestrians could shoot at you with pistols as you blasted by.

There. Yes. Movement.

The wreck was twisting like a fish on a hook, fighting him.

Stupid swordfish didn't have as much patience as Del. No fish did.

He reached out with his right hand, keeping the left ready on the thrusters, and tweaked the nose of his steed around to the left just a hair. Not even a degree. Maybe an arc-second.

Something broke.

Good broke, not bad broke. Nothing like bad touch.

The wreck groaned. Or the cable. Or this sub.

Forward movement lurched through the entire construct.

Del listened to the gods singing.

He cut power to nothing and then brought it back up with a vertical as the cable snapped him back towards the wreck.

Never do to slam into it and undo everything he'd just achieved.

"Ilan, gimme status," Del hollered as he brought everything to rest.

"Not bad, old man," Lead Machinist Ilan Yu said. "Ten degrees off vertical, give or take. Moving in now to unfoul the cable. You hold position while me and the Captain work."

Cheers went up from the back of the room. Del suddenly remembered that he had passengers besides Bethany. Somebody clapped a hand on his shoulder.

Del looked up, but didn't recognize the man.

"Thank you," the guy said with tears rolling down his face.

Del didn't get it, but smiled and nodded. He had no idea what had happened down here before he'd arrived.

Must have been good.

The others were there, too. Happy faces made Del feel like his own personal demigod.

But now the hard part.

PART TWO

Ilan was back at *Nidavellir*, just like his nightmares that were never far from the surface when he went to sleep.

Back in that life pod, blasting clear of the about-to-be-blown-up transport. Just before somebody opened fire on them and nearly hit, scoring a corner close enough to bombard the interior with shrapnel.

And that one sword that had impaled Afia.

Ilan turned the heat up another notch as the interior of his dive armor just didn't seem to want to keep him warm. He wasn't sure that anything could at this point.

He was back in a waking nightmare.

He just had to remind himself that Afia had survived. Was over on the submarine right now, safe and sound and probably laughing and cheering another impossible escape with the Science Officer.

Ilan had no idea how Javier's luck worked, he was just happy to be close enough to it for some to rub off occasionally. He was going to need it.

Thruster pack on, he started to close.

"Follow my lead," he instructed the Captain, feeling a little ridiculous, but that couldn't be helped.

Afia was the combat engineer, but they didn't have a suit her size. Ilan was next in skill and seniority. Sokolov just happened to be handy, else Ilan would have done all this alone.

Maybe having the Captain along wasn't so bad, then.

They closed.

The wreckage stood more or less upright now. Exterior lights were on, framing the outline well, but the only interior lights on this side were on the top deck cabins.

Ilan glanced over and made sure Sokolov was close by as he got up to the side of the wreckage.

Second deck. According to Javier and Afia, this was where the vessel's crew had bunked, with all the engineering spaces below that.

Ilan ground his teeth together and put his helmet light to the porthole in front of him, illuminating the interior.

He'd seen dead people before. Never killed someone, but the ship had been in a bad business for a long time before Javier came along, and it had been an occupational hazard.

Two dead guys in here. Looked like they had opened the cabin door when those bombs went off and couldn't get them closed again before the flood waters claimed them.

Ilan had always thought that dying in a vacuum would be about the worst way to go, but the face floating nearby just took him right back to that escape pod.

"You okay?" Captain Sokolov's voice came across.

Ilan didn't think he'd made a sound. Maybe the man had seen a flinch all the way through the dive armor or something.

"Fine," Ilan lied, moving on to the next window.

It probably wasn't obvious from the interior, but he could see where the hull had flexed pretty hard. The exterior line was maybe five degrees out of true.

Slamming into a mountain in free fall?

The next chamber was filled with dead guys and wreckage. Ilan wondered if the frame had kinked and sprung leaks. With as much pressure as they had outside, it wouldn't take much for a weld to fail and then you were dead.

Leaks in the dyke. The only question would be fast or slow.

And he didn't have enough cloth tape. There might not be enough in the galaxy at that point.

A hand tapped his helmet.

Ilan flinched again and turned.

Sokolov was right there. The man pulled Ilan's face plate against his.

"You can do this, Ilan," Captain Sokolov said slowly and clearly.

Radio was off. Private message.

The Captain believes in you.

Ilan fought back tears and nodded.

Back at *Nidavellir*, elbow deep in Afia's blood, trying to save her life.

Deep breath. Shallow the breathing.

You can do this.

But they were all dead here.

Not a surprise. This side had been dark. He worked his way around the aft of the wreckage and got to the damaged side.

Plasma lance explosives. Shaped charge attached to the exterior of the hull. Bastard went after frames and decks. Two bombs. Two holes. Rear two thirds of the starboard side of decks two and three were open to death pressure.

Crush pressure.

Whatever you called it when the ocean would kill you like a gnat.

There was a light on in the forward-most cabin on this deck. The first he'd seen.

It had been down in the mud earlier, or the inhabitant hadn't bothered turning the light on as he waited to die.

God, was there anything worse than dying alone in an inescapable box?

Ilan shined his light in the window anyway and saw a man's face from two meters away.

That was what hope looked like. That moment when the Dragoon arrived with help and took charge of getting Afia back to sick bay where the robot surgeon could keep her alive.

Ilan waved, knowing what that face contained. The figure waved back.

One man, trapped in a tiny chamber no bigger than the one Ilan had slept in, back aboard *Storm Gauntlet* when he was a fresh punk. As opposed to a senior punk today.

Crush pressure on all sides. Trapped in a single room with a single layer of metal on all sides.

Hope.

He would get exactly one chance at this.

They were all back at *Nidavellir*.

Ilan turned.

"Captain Sokolov, I need you to board the submarine," Ilan said.

"Negative," the man replied. "I'll stay outside to help."

"I gave you an order, sailor," Ilan snapped. "Execute it."

Sokolov flinched. Back on the bridge with Javier, the others listening probably did, too.

Ilan didn't think he sounded human right now. Might not be.

Sokolov started to reply, caught himself, and nodded. Turning, the man backed away a distance for pickup.

"Del, this is Ilan," he continued when he thought he could sound rational.

"Talk to me, kid," the pilot replied instantly.

"You pick up Sokolov and airlock him aboard," Ilan said. "Then I need you to maneuver yourself around to me where I'm standing."

"Stand by," Del said.

Ilan reached out an armored hand and put it flat against the window. Inside, the other man did the same.

Hope, instead of a slow death.

If this worked.

If it didn't, at least it would probably be a fast death at this depth.

They waited.

Del approached like a whale coming out of the darkness once Sokolov was out of the way. Ilan turned his back to the wreckage and started calling maneuvering vectors over the radio.

"Down one meter, your left sixty centimeters," he said slowly, patiently, clearly. "Approach another three meters and hold."

The main airlock mocked him like a whale's mouth opening to swallow him whole now.

"Stabilize there," Ilan said. "Javier, I need you to get into the survival supplies and dig out all the spray foam sealant cans. Airlock them through to the outside but nobody comes out with them. Am I clear?"

The pause before the Science Officer replied was telling, but Ilan wasn't asking for favors or help. This was his mission now.

"Spray foam in the lock," Javier said. "Lock open to ocean. Stand by."

Ilan turned halfway back. Enough to keep an eye on the sub while also being able to wave to the last survivor.

The airlock closed. Pumps began emptying the chamber with a surge of bubbles on all sides.

Ilan waved and gave the man a thumb's up, hoping he was communicating that he knew what he was doing.

Ilan hoped he knew what he was doing.

The outer hatch opened again and Ilan stepped into the airlock.

The cans were strong enough to survive for a while. They were meant to be used in a vacuum to seal cracks and breaks and made of the same stuff you built hulls from. Probably lacked the structural strength he needed, but Ilan didn't need it to last long.

"Del, we're going to do this with a modified soft seal environment," Ilan called. "Maintain all vectors and shift yourself two meters closer to the wreckage."

"Coming up, kid," Del replied.

The submarine oozed closer by centimeters.

Everyone always assumed Del was crazy. They always forgot that he was also that good. The submarine came right up to the edge and held.

"Forward another ten centimeters and up ten," Ilan called.

The submarine carried him right up to the edge of the wreck.

"Rotate your bow around just enough that it moves the right side six centimeters closer without the left moving," Ilan continued.

Magic happened.

But it was Del. He was good at that.

"Del, deploy the soft seal fringe," Ilan ordered.

"Coming up."

Ilan could tell that the man wanted to ask questions. Was just begging to know if it would work.

They would find out in about three minutes.

"Okay, I have soft seal," Ilan announced as the edges of the airlock pushed out and deployed.

You needed something like this when you didn't have matching airlocks. *Balustrade* did their designs weird, maybe on purpose. Different dimensions from everybody else, so they added what Ilan could only think of as lips around the outside, to let you give a ship a hickey or something.

"Del, I need you to give me just enough thruster power to hold you against the side of the wreckage, exactly on this vector, without pushing anything over," Ilan continued. "Am I clear?"

"Roger that," Del grunted. "Kid, you're even crazier than Javier. Glad I lived long enough to even see somebody try this stunt."

Ilan shook his head.

Nidavellir. They weren't home yet.

The hull changed pitch around him and hummed.

Here goes nothing.

Ilan picked up the first can and sprayed the point where the airlock seal and the hull of the other vessel touched. The stuff barely foamed at all, but again, he didn't need it for long.

All around the outside. A second time. A third, because he was feeling paranoid.

Empty cans save one.

Do. Or die.

"Del, I am triggering the lock cycle," Ilan said. "Somebody override the doors so they don't close on me in the middle of this shit."

"I have you, Ilan," a woman's voice came back.

Not one he recognized immediately, so that must be the new Historian Javier had hired. Durbin. She must be Del's co-pilot today.

Weird, but Del wouldn't want an amateur, so she must be good.

He reached out and told the system to pump all the water out of the chamber.

Slowly, the system succeeded. One spot sprang a leak and Ilan hit it with more spray foam. This actually did something, so the pressure in here must be low enough.

Sure hurt like hell now to move this dive armor. Need to have Javier spring for a full exosuit next time.

Mostly dry.

Dry enough.

Launch the escape pod.

Except he wasn't back at *Nidavellir*. This was *Ugen*. New nightmare, maybe, but he'd saved Afia then.

He could save this guy now.

Ilan reached onto his belt and pulled out the rescue hammer. Instead of a blunt head, it came down to a chisel tip. You shattered something like dive glass or a ship's portal by overloading one tiny point with all the weight you could put behind it.

He gestured the other guy to back away from the window. Fellow had a look of incredulity on his face, but Ilan didn't know if it would work, either.

Step forward. Pivot a little.

Hit the window like you did that station. Kill it with one unstoppable blow.

The glass started to surrender.

Hit it again. A third time.

The pieces disintegrated now, held in place by a polymer coating designed to be your last resort.

Ilan flipped the hammer around and got the cutting edge into a gap, pulling hard as he stepped back.

The window failed.

Around him, Ilan watched the ocean probe the edges of the soft seal and spray, trying to get in and kill the guy. There wasn't much time before everything failed.

Rather than anything fancy, Ilan just stuck a hand into the hole and pulled the rest of it out of the sill in chunks. Wasn't like he needed it for anything, and they didn't award bonus points for neatness here.

Ilan gestured and stepped back. The man clambered through the window awkwardly. He might have been talking, but Ilan had the outside pickups off. Too much noise already.

The man stepped close and hugged him, slimy dive armor and all, in the tight confines of the airlock.

Ilan laughed and triggered the outer lock doors closed.

Ugen, not *Nidavellir*.

PART THREE

JAVIER MADE sure he was first in line outside the inner airlock hatch when it opened. He more or less pulled the guy named Hassan past him and handed the fellow off to Afia and the others for medical inspection.

He wanted to see the other man.

Ilan had the helmet unscrewed and off now, hanging next to Zakhar's on the rack.

The kid's face looked like someone had pulled him backwards through a knothole in a fence, but the smile was bigger than anything Javier could remember.

"Ya done good," Javier stepped close and put a hand on the shoulder of the armor.

"Had a pretty good teacher," Ilan laughed. "No dead Norwegian rats this time, though."

Javier laughed with him.

First time he had ever laid eyes on a punk named Ilan Yu had been to sit on the far side of the room, handcuffed, and walk a junior, aspiring Machinist's Mate with four months of self-taught education through the process of how to clean out part of the life support system.

Including a dead rat.

Ilan started on other panels of the armor, so Javier reached out and started unclipping buckles and locks.

"Nobody else?" Javier asked in a much quieter voice as the noise outside ramped up.

Javier knew everyone wanted to celebrate, but they were letting him have this moment with his second oldest friend in the entire crew, after only Suvi herself.

"Checked every porthole, like you taught me, Javier," Ilan replied in a quiet voice as well, filled with an immensity of pain Javier understood.

Ilan hadn't ever talked about *Nidavellir* with anybody else but him, as far as Javier knew. *Hammerfield* and *Storm Gauntlet* hadn't ever had a Ship's Psychologist or even a Chaplain, who could have worked with folks recovering from trauma. 'Mina Teague was about as close as they'd ever gotten, and she'd only been with the crew for a couple of months before heading out on her own adventures in the modern age, five hundred years after she'd been lost forever at sea in her own way.

Breastplate came clear and the winch hooks pulled it up and out of the way. Ilan sat back onto the bench and grabbed the bar to pull himself up out of the legs.

Ilan looked more like himself and less like a bizarre, aquatic God of War at that point.

There was still pain in his eyes, but hope as well.

Javier smiled.

"Now what, Javier?" he asked.

Javier could have answered the obvious question with something like *We're going home* but that wasn't what Ilan wanted to know.

From the agony in his eyes, the kid had seen the rest of the crew. Or at least enough of them to know that Hassan was the last one ever getting out alive. Him and Magee were it from the lower decks, and then only because Ilan Yu had turned into a pretty good engineer.

"Now we get to the surface and rendezvous with the rest of *The Lander*," Javier replied grimly. "And then we go rattle some cages."

"Only one significant station in orbit," Ilan observed in a voice utterly drained of emotion.

"Not going to kill anybody, Ilan," Javier nodded. "Most of them are innocent civilians this time. Hopefully, we never have to kill another station again, you and I."

"Then what?"

"This was an assassination attempt, Ilan," Javier growled. "Would have succeeded but for Suvi, Del, and you. We'd all have died in another twenty-four hours or so. Long before rescue subs might have realized we'd gone missing and started looking for us. I have a theory as to who did it."

"I'll help," Ilan said.

"You don't even know what I have planned," Javier replied.

"You didn't look in windows to see dead men and women, Javier," Ilan snapped. "To count them, hoping that there might be somebody other than Hassan we could somehow rescue. Somebody deserves to be fed to the ish in small pieces for that."

"We're the good guys now, Ilan."

"I don't care, Javier," Ilan stood up and got right into Javier's face.

The kid was still shorter, and barefoot at that, but his heart was in the right place. And his soul.

"Oh, I didn't say he was getting away with it, kid," Javier smiled grimly now. He stepped back out of the airlock and gestured Ilan to join him. "Plus, I got some folks here who'd like to say thank you."

Javier stepped clear as Afia grabbed the guy in a pixie bearhug and lifted him up off the deck. The other women were there a moment later, including Bethany, but she was the only one who didn't kiss Ilan.

Djamila's was the one that made the kid blush.

Javier walked over and sat down next to Andak, opposite Isaboe.

"I heard what you said," Andak commented neutrally. "Now what?"

"Now, I have footage that Del shot of the wreck," Javier said. "And the coordinates so that you can send a retrieval team here to bring the other bodies home and see what someone did to you. And Ambassadorial credentials, but I'm not going to just walk up and shoot Fritz in the face with them."

"We would have to throw you off the planet for that," Andak nodded with the slightest trace of a grin. "And revoke your diplomatic immunity."

Javier grunted. Wasn't *quite* worth it.

Yet.

"So instead, I'm going to give an interview to whoever wants to chat," Javier grinned. "My diplomatic immunity also shields me against libel and slander. And once you bring your yacht home, I'd really like Fritz Bamanie to try to sue me, just so I can drag his ass into court and subject his entire freaking life to *discovery* by a pack of rabid lawyers with a blank check."

Even Andak shuddered at that. Fates worse than death, and all that, with businessmen like this.

Javier nodded and rose, walking over now to where Del was pretending to be all cool and stuff.

Javier shook the old flyer's hand and took the co-pilot seat.

"You ready?" he asked.

"Thought you'd never ask," Del laughed and brought the bow up and around as the thrusters engaged.

PART FOUR

DEL STUDIED the surface as he broached. Storm coming in from the west, but nothing bad as yet. Three meter seas would make the ride a little rough, but they'd practiced in worse on *Altai*, just to understand how to do this.

"Dom, what is your location?" Del asked the radio.

"Above and north of you," Mikhail Dominguez answered a moment later. "We have company, but I ordered them all out of my landing zone to a radius of three kilometers."

Del nodded. Not enough to keep someone from suddenly rushing and strafing, if they were serious about making a second assassination attempt, but it would give him clear skies to work while they could see what was going on.

"Roger that," Del called back. He glanced over at Javier. "You wanna do this?"

"Your ship, your rescue," Javier grinned. "Plus, I can blame you if something goes wrong."

Del grumbled a few obscenities far enough under his breath that the rest of the passengers didn't hear them and then activated the targeting beacons.

"Dom, loop west for your approach," Del said. "I'll turn ass into the storm so I'm running with the waves."

"Stand by, Del."

He watched on the radar as the outer shell they were

allowed to call *The Lander* when he wasn't flying it came around and started to close. The waves were running on a bizarre harmonic of ten and one hundred, rather than the eight and sixty-four common on many worlds. Something about the shape of the floor beneath him, he supposed.

"One hundred and shallow, Dom," Del called. "Make your first run."

"Coming in now."

The Lander had deployed the claw on all four cables. Dom settled on thrusters and began manipulating things. Del's job was to hold his craft as perfectly still, relative, as conditions would allow.

"Dom, shift right about a meter," Javier suddenly said. "Count to eight and then be ready to latch us."

Del grunted, but he'd been focused on the sky, not the waves. Javier must have seen something coming.

Overhead, the shadows changed as the kid maneuvered.

Clunk.

Boy howdy, first try?

Hell, they hadn't been able to do that on Altai.

"Got you." Dom sounded almost surprised, but what the hell.

"Land and reel me in," Del said.

The shell settled like a con game on a busy street and Del was looking at the interior of *The Lander*'s bay, instead of sky. More thumps and clunks as various pieces locked onto the beacons and then grabbed hold everywhere.

Del shut his engines down now and listened as Dom closed the outer hatch, sealing them in with whatever dumbass cephalopods or anglerfish had been too dumb to let go earlier. Maybe he needed to start an aquarium, instead of just dumping them to deep space when he got back to orbit?

"Suvi, we're docked," Javier announced on the general line. "Ask Piet to sound General Quarters."

"Stand by," she replied on the central screen.

"Was that really necessary?" Del turned to ask Javier, since he was done flying for now.

Well, he could go upstairs and evict Dom, claiming seniority or something, but the kid had done a fine job holding the horses while Del and the others went off and had a rescue adventure, so it would be kinda rude.

"Necessary?" Javier shrugged. "Appropriate, all things considered? You betcha."

"You think somebody's feeling that frisky?" Del asked.

"If he is, I want someone else to remind them that I'm the same guy that did *Nidavellir*," Zakhar suddenly spoke up.

Damn captain had snuck up on him. Again.

Del cranked his shoulders all the way around.

"We need to kill folks to get home?" he asked the two of them pointedly.

"We'll see," Javier answered in a cold, ugly tone.

"Well, shit, then."

Del unbuckled and rose from his seat.

"Where are you going?" Zakhar asked.

"Dom's gonna need a copilot up there if you folks haven't had enough adventure for one day."

PART FIVE

JAVIER STUDIED the view on the screen. Zakhar and Djamila had gone upstairs, providing Del and Dom a command officer and a turret gunner, respectively.

Excalibur was growing ever larger as he watched.

"We could have gone to the station directly," Andak offered from the other seat. "Or the main dome. Why do we need to go aboard your warship first?"

"I'm about to make a series of reckless and provocatory accusations on an unsecured comm line, possibly in the course of being interviewed by the evening news on our daring escape from an assassin, Andak," Javier replied.

"So you want to be protected?" the man asked.

"I want to be remote enough that I don't punch somebody in the nose," he retorted. "Don't knock them down and then stomp their skull to make my point."

He glanced over and noted that the man had gone a little gray again. But then, Andak Luo had been born rich, unlike everyone else on this vessel. His battles had probably never included anything more personally dangerous than a rabid lawyer.

Certainly never been shot at by someone good enough to do the job.

"Then what?" Andak asked after a long stretch of silence.

"Then I'm probably going to make sure there is enough evidence of malfeasance on public record to destroy somebody," Javier said. "After that, I figure it would be best for everyone if *Excalibur* went elsewhere. Normally I'd invite you along to see the sights, but you and Lan need to be here, cleaning up the mess I'm about to leave behind. I'd do it myself, but there's no way I don't make it worse trying."

"You coming back?" Andak asked. "Still got trade and stuff to talk about. That long term mission you talked about, linking places like *Ugen* with *Altai*, clear around the wheel."

"In a while," Javier said. "Emma and Rainier are technically supposed to be taken home in eight months, but have already let me know they'd like to extend their mission for another school year. Their university won't complain, since I'm paying their salary plus a stipend to the school."

"So where's the next stop?" Andak asked.

"*Trotau Skale*," Javier replied. "Another world a lot more like *Earth*, with serious oceans to explore. Picked them up on a Gazetteer map I bought at *Dreely*."

"They need a hero, too?" Andak laughed. "An old style gunslinger who comes into town and disrupts everything, saving the day before he rides off into the sunset?"

"Everybody does, Andak," Javier smiled at the man. "Most of them just don't understand that ahead of time."

ABOUT THE AUTHOR

Blaze Ward writes science fiction in the Alexandria Station universe (Jessica Keller, The Science Officer, The Story Road, etc.) as well as several other science fiction universes, such as Star Dragon, the Dominion, and more. He also writes odd bits of high fantasy with swords and orcs. In addition, he is the Editor and Publisher of *Boundary Shock Quarterly Magazine*. You can find out more at his website www.blazeward.com, as well as Facebook, Goodreads, and other places.

Blaze's works are available as ebooks, paper, and audio, and can be found at a variety of online vendors. His newsletter comes out regularly, and you can also follow his blog on his website. He really enjoys interacting with fans, and looks forward to any and all questions—even ones about his books!

Never miss a release!
If you'd like to be notified of new releases, sign up for my newsletter.

http://www.blazeward.com/newsletter/

Buy More!
Did you know that you can buy directly from my website?

https://www.blazeward.com/shop/

Connect with Blaze!

Web: www.blazeward.com

Boundary Shock Quarterly (BSQ):
https://www.boundaryshockquarterly.com/

ABOUT KNOTTED ROAD PRESS

Knotted Road Press fiction specializes in dynamic writing set in mysterious, exotic locations.

Knotted Road Press non–fiction publishes autobiographies, business books, cookbooks, and how–to books with unique voices.

Knotted Road Press creates DRM–free ebooks as well as high–quality print books for readers around the world.

With authors in a variety of genres including literary, poetry, mystery, fantasy, and science fiction, Knotted Road Press has something for everyone.

Knotted Road Press
www.KnottedRoadPress.com